YA

the
BETRAYAL
of Natalie Hargrove

the
BETRAYAL
of Natalie Hargrove

LAUREN KATE

razOr
bill

AN IMPRINT OF PENGUIN GROUP (USA) INC

The Betrayal of Natalie Hargrove

RAZORBILL

Published by the Penguin Group
Penguin Young Readers Group
345 Hudson Street, New York, New York 10014, U.S.A.
Penguin Group (USA) Inc., 375 Hudson Street, New York, New York 10014, U.S.A.
Penguin Group (Canada), 90 Eglinton Avenue East, Suite 700, Toronto, Ontario,
Canada M4P 2Y3 (a division of Pearson Penguin Canada Inc.)
Penguin Books Ltd, 80 Strand, London WC2R 0RL, England
Penguin Ireland, 25 St Stephen's Green, Dublin 2, Ireland (a division of Penguin Books Ltd)
Penguin Group (Australia), 250 Camberwell Road, Camberwell, Victoria 3124,
Australia (a division of Pearson Australia Group Pty Ltd)
Penguin Books India Pvt Ltd, 11 Community Centre,
Panchsheel Park, New Delhi – 110 017, India
Penguin Group (NZ), 67 Apollo Drive, Rosedale, North Shore 0632, New Zealand
(a division of Pearson New Zealand Ltd.)
Penguin Books (South Africa) (Pty) Ltd, 24 Sturdee Avenue, Rosebank,
Johannesburg 2196, South Africa

Penguin Books Ltd, Registered Offices: 80 Strand, London WC2R 0RL, England

10 9 8 7 6 5 4 3 2 1

Library of Congress Cataloging-in-Publication Data
Kate, Lauren
The betrayal of Natalie Hargrove / Lauren Kate.
p. cm.

Summary: South Carolina high school senior Nat has worked hard to put her
trailer-park past behind her, and when she and her boyfriend are crowned
Palmetto Prince and Princess everything would be perfect, except that a prank
they played a few nights before went horribly awry.
ISBN: 9781595142658
[1. Secrets—Fiction. 2. Social classes—Fiction. 3. Contests—Fiction. 4. High schools—Fiction.
5. Schools—Fiction. 6. Charleston (S.C.)—Fiction.] 1. Title
PZ7.K15655 Bet 2009
[Fic] 22

2009018481

Printed in the United States of America

FOR JASON,
CO-CONSPIRATOR

Prologue

Once upon a time, you knew nothing.

It wasn't your fault—you were just a kid. And growing up where you did, most people assumed that this was for the best. The longer it took a small town southern girl to catch on to the backward ways of her world, the better off everyone was.

Back then, your biggest worries were not getting caught stealing that pack of Juicy Fruit from the drugstore . . . oh, and making it out of elementary school with some semblance of a soul.

The danger was real. Remember that dress code? The mid-calf-length pleated pea-green skirts? Remember your troll . . . er, role models? Every last one of your teachers was of the dingy-slip-wearing, needs-to-Nair-her-mustache, hasn't-gotten-laid-in-your-lifetime variety. It took everything in you to stay awake as year after year, they stood up at the board, rattling off the titillating trivia of your state.

South Carolina, you'd jotted. *Eighth state to sign the Constitution. Home of the Palmetto tree, the golden wren, the yellow Jessamine, the saccharine social climber*—oh wait, that one wasn't on the test (not yet, anyway).

If you were anything like Natalie Hargrove, you couldn't have cared less if you passed or failed that week's pop quiz. But what they don't tell you in Dixie is that one day down the line, something as benign as the South Carolina state tree just might be a matter of life and death.

CHAPTER *One*

SOMETHING WICKED THIS WAY COMES

*I*t was the biggest week of my life. It was ten minutes before the bell. I was perched outside the sophomore bathroom door, honing one of my very favorite skills. Oh, *eavesdropping* is *such* an ugly word! Especially when I make it look so good. Admit it: the decoy cell phone at my ear, the coolly absorbed look on my face—I had you convinced that I was just retrieving some private late-night message from Mike, or double-checking the pre-party details for Rex Freeman's Mardi Gras soiree this weekend. Didn't I?

But when were things at Palmetto High ever really what they seemed? Anyone with a pulse knew that the sophomore girls a.k.a. the Bambies—were the go-to playthings of the senior boys. The few of us at this school lucky enough to be blessed with a brain had figured out by now that the Bambi morning primp sessions were seriously ripe for eavesdropping. Bambi-bathroom-perching was merely precautionary, to keep oneself in the know.

Through the door, in between bursts of omnious-sounding thunder from the storm brewing outside, I made out some Bambi whining: "Can we discuss how unfair it is that this weather is so foul?" February in Charleston was particularly unpredictable. Black clouds had hovered all morning, threatening to open up at any moment and drown us.

"It's like God wants our hair to pouf at the game tonight," her Bambi friend agreed. "Hey—who took my concealer?"

"Honey," a third Bambi drawled. "Next week's church bells are too far away for you to be all godded up already. Pass the Citre Shine."

Christ, these girls were a drag. If I wanted to get anything good out of them (read: whom the senior boys were rallying behind for next week's long awaited Palmetto Court vote), I was going to have to go in there myself. I flipped my phone shut and gave my stage smile to the polyamorous thespians passing me in the hall. Then I sidled through the bathroom doorway.

Inside Bambiland, I raised my eyebrows, pursed my lips, and stepped into a cloud of orange-scented hairspray to butt my way in front of their mirror.

"Sophomores," I said. "Move."

After a chorus of *Hi Natalie's,* and *Sorry Natalie's,* the Bambies shut their mouths and stepped aside. All talk of the storm clouds and subsequent hair frizz seemed to be forgotten.

Even Kate Richards, sophomore ringleader and the least objectionable of the bunch, put down her curling iron to scooch over. Kate had earned her street cred with me during her freshmen haze last year when a senior handed her a pair of scissors and asked Kate to show her respect by sacrificing her waist-length locks. Half my class still hadn't gotten over Kate's great defiance when she stormed out of her own haze, but personally, I had to respect a girl with that much verve.

This morning, Kate knew—as they all knew—that it wasn't like a senior to primp on Bambi turf. In one fell swoop, she stacked her entire clique's cosmetic cases in the crook of her arm and cleared a space for me on the countertop. I winked my thanks and she winked back, tossing the curled portion of her now-famous honey-colored hair over one shoulder. Casually, I plunked down my own cosmetic case. I glanced in the mirror. My dark hair fell effortlessly around my shoulders, making my dark brown eyes shine. My skin was smooth and clear. But there was an annoying worry wrinkle right in the middle of my forehead. I took another breath and pulled out my eyelash curler.

Through the one eye not clamped by what Mike called my medieval torture device, I surveyed my effect on the now-silent scene.

"What's the matter, girls?" I said, turning my back to Kate so she'd know I wasn't implicating her. "Nat got your tongue?"

Steph Merritt, your basic sophomore born-again blonde, looked at her feet and stammered. "We were just talking about how much we love your Palmetto Court posters, Nat."

"Were you?" I asked.

Steph's button nose flared in alarm. Normally, I respected a little white lie—a girl had to do what a girl had to do—but today Steph's faux flattery was as low rate as her dye job. Before I made my presence known, these girls had been totally consumed by their ratty hair and acne. If the guys they were banging had mentioned anything about how they were casting their votes, the Bambies were probably too stupid to remember. Yes, they were sleeping with the enemy, but at their age, one senior football player just blended right into the next.

I hated wasting time before the bell rang. By the time my mascara dried, I knew I was going to have to get my information elsewhere.

The junior class definitely wasn't as tight with the senior guys as the Bambies were. Juniors were hot, but too new-agey for their own good, and they usually hung around in the low-country marshland with scruffy out-of-towner guys who drove minicampers stocked with all-you-could-puff vaporizers.

Then again, strange things *had* been known to go on in their bathroom before school hours. There were rumors that the crème of their class had predicted when Lanie Dougherty would lose her virginity—down to the hour—and been right. And just last month, those very same juniors had been the first to know about the whole mortifying embezzlement scandal that got Principal Duncan fired and replaced with the temporary and painfully dweebish Principal Glass.

In the mirror behind me, Darla Duke stood picking at a large red zit in her T-zone. Believe me when I say that the Double D didn't just rub me the wrong way because her father was dating my mother. With her bacne, permanent brown nose, and all-too-visible cleavage, the girl was legitimately gross. When she caught me watching her zit-pick with my eyebrows raised in horror, the way a vegetarian might look at, say, pork gristle, she dropped her hands to her sides.

I popped open my Mary Kay compact and dabbed the pink pouf around my nose. "Don't worry, D," I said. "It might clear up by this afternoon."

The sophomores gasped. There was nothing polite about mentioning another girl's blemish, even in the privacy of the powder room.

I rolled my eyes. "I mean, the weather."

Outside, thunder rolled. Strands of weeping willows slapped the windows, and the sophomores whined and pulled on their hair in unison. It was embarrassing, watching them all wig out over a few insignificant flyaways before a pep rally. How did they expect to cut it in two years when there were legitimate things to stress about? I sighed and pulled a bottle of my secret weapon hair gloss, courtesy of Mom, from my purple backpack. I didn't need to court votes from these girls, but around here, you could catch a lot of flies with really good hair products.

"Promise to share?" I asked the sophomores, waving the bottle in the air.

The Human Blemish held out her hands as if I'd just spun gold. "Oh my God, thank you," Darla blinked. "We'll each take just one spritz."

"Right," I said, heading for the door. "Don't go *too* crazy."

"Nat." Kate's throaty voice stood out among the other girls' chirps. She tugged on the strap of my bag. "Wait up."

"Talk to me." I turned around to straighten the collar of her white oxford shirt so that it lay smoothly under her pale-pink cashmere.

"Tracy Lampert wants to see you," she said, flashing the silver tongue ring she hardly ever let show on school grounds. "Junior bathroom," Kate directed. "Before the bell."

Hmm . . . Tracy Lampert was the self-appointed junior-class guru. She held perpetual court in their bathroom, to the point where some wondered if she ever went to class.

"That's convenient," I said, wondering briefly about the odds. Tracy and I were cool, but I couldn't remember the last time we'd sought out each other's company—simultaneously. "I was on my way up there, anyway," I said, shrugging good-bye to the rest of the Bambies. "Later, girls."

As I slipped up the stairs toward Tracy's Den of Zen, I was surprised to see how suddenly inundated the halls were with my running mates' Palmetto Ball Court posters. Taking all of them in, I started to laugh—not just because someone had convinced June Rattler to blow up a red-faced, puffy-cheeked photo of herself honking on a tuba for her Palmetto Princess Poster, though that was pretty hilarious—and vaguely disturbing. No, I started laughing because in a weird way, it felt good to realize that I wasn't the only one consumed by thoughts of the crown.

Here's how crazy Palmetto is about its Ball: For one month every year, hippies forget their vows to reduce their carbon imprint and sit around their bonfires high as kites, making just as many glittery posters as the rest of us. Tramps start wearing underwear and going back to church to grease the moral judges who make the final call. Former-Princesses-turned-parents habitually bribe the school with donations of new library wings to ensure their own children's royal legacies. Even the boys go on celery-hot-sauce diets to drop a few pounds before their campaign photo shoots.

Yes, the guys take it that seriously, too. Unless, of course, we're talking about my boyfriend. I love him, okay? I do. Mike and I are undoubtedly the school's most-likely-to-succeed couple. All I'm saying is if everyone in the world could get away with caring about certain things as little as Mike does . . . well, there just might not be a Palmetto Court Campaign at all.

And the campaign is only the beginning! After the ballots are cast and the winners announced, the real reign of Palmetto Prince and Princess begins. "Royalty" at Palmetto means you're a cross between ambassador of goodwill and highest-ranking socialite. Basically: You've arrived.

To celebrate, the whole school throws you a massive weeklong party. First, there's the country club coronation—to which the Prince and Princess arrive by a glittering horse and carriage. Then there's the Jessamine Day—where all the girls sport their glorified state-flower corsages. There's the famous "Path to Palmetto" video, widely distributed, and known to have gotten more than a few former Royals into their choice of Ivy Leagues. Finally, of course, there's the Ball.

"Gimme a countdown to the Ball—go!" Rex Freeman's voice rang out through the hall. Rex, with his buzzed red hair and biceps always bulging through his rolled up T-shirt sleeves, was way more laid-back than he looked at the moment. Usually, he was only a taskmaster when it came to getting the right number of kegs to his parties. But from the panicked expression of his lanky sophomore assistant, Rex was taking his job as Campaign Commissioner pretty seriously this year.

"Did I stutter?" he barked at the kid. "I asked you how many days."

"Guh . . . fifteen," the boy twittered, backing against his locker.

"And how many posters per Prince are allowed on the walls fifteen days out?" Rex barked.

As the sophomore flipped frantically through a stapled packet of rules and regulations, Rex looked up and grinned at me.

"I assume your poster count is in compliance ma'am," he joked, putting on his hick Carolina officer-of-the-law voice and giving my shoulder a squeeze.

"Oh, you know I play by the rules, officer," I quipped back, matching his southern accent with my best damsel-in-distress.

"That's more than I can say for your boyfriend," Rex winced, looking down at his biceps. "I might need a witch doctor after Mike's tackle today."

I groaned and popped a piece of Juicy Fruit in my mouth. Rex and Mike had been tight since they accidentally tied their shoelaces together back in second grade, so I was used to them horsing around. But this week was no time to get a stupid football injury!

Usually, I love Mike's carefree-yet-successful way of going about high school—he definitely balanced me out. But Mike's place on the Court should have been just as much of a shoo-in as mine this year. It would be, too, if he'd just put in the tiniest bit of effort—well, and if it weren't for Justin Balmer.

I leaned over to tap the packet Rex's lackey was still fumbling through. "If I were you, I'd keep an eye on J.B.'s poster count," I said before continuing down the hall.

Of all the posters plastered on the wall, Justin's was the one I knew I'd be most unnerved by—so I'd made myself promise to avoid it. I was this close to reaching the junior bathroom safely when I came face to face with J.B.'s cardboard incarnation and stopped dead in my tracks.

In the picture, Justin stood tan and shirtless on one of his boats in his father's marina down near Folly Beach. And okay, it wasn't an entirely unattractive photo. In fact, the intense look in his deep-green eyes almost made me stumble forward. When I leaned in for a closer look, I realized I knew that boat. I'd once spent an endless evening on it back when . . . well, back when things were different.

Justin Balmer, the poster read, *a Prince eighteen years in the making.*

Please, more like eighteen years in the faking. I'd learned the hard way that J.B. was so much less than the sum of his cotillioned parts. You'd be hard-pressed to find a bigger

the BETRAYAL of Natalie Hargrove

sham—and at Palmetto, that was saying something. I squinted at the picture, wondering which Bambi skank had taken it, and when.

"I thought you gave up idol worship." It was Justin, leaning against the wall and smirking at me with those same green eyes. He smelled the way he always did—Kiehl's aftershave and freshly cut grass.

I gestured at the poster, unimpressed. "I was just checking to see whether that was a smudge or a giant mole on your chest," I said. "Have you put on some weight?"

"Cute cover up, Nat," he said in a low voice. "But I think we already know all about each other's secret charming imperfections." His hand grazed the small of my back, just inside the waist of my jeans.

I shoved him back against the locker, then quickly spun around to check for witnesses. I did not want anyone seeing me sweat Justin Balmer in plain sight. Luckily, the only person in the hallway was bespectacled Ari Ang, who scurried by carrying a beaker full of something green.

"I didn't see anything," the Anger pleaded, covering his large-frame glasses with his beaker. "I'm just on my way to chemistry. . . ." His voice trailed off, and I turned back around to face Justin.

Once, we might have laughed about the Anger's perpetual beaker handling. Now I wanted to spit my new piece of Juicy

Fruit in J.B.'s face. But I made myself swallow the bilious instinct. I forced a smile.

"Aww," I cooed. "It's cute that you still think your—what was your phrase—charming imperfections are secret." I let my eyes pause deliberately on his crotch before spitting out my gum, tearing off a piece of Justin's poster, and wadding the yellow sphere inside it. "Don't worry," I went on, "my lips were sealed. But if you ever want to really check in with yourself, try hacking into the Bambi blog about you—and maybe stop slutting yourself out quite so much. Those girls are merciless. See ya."

"Nat," he grabbed my wrist, forcing me to look him in the eye. "Come on."

"Come on what?"

"Can't a guy change?" he asked so quietly I had to lean in to hear.

I hung there, knowing the answer like I knew my own name: no. But I couldn't make myself respond. Finally, I settled for whipping my hand away and ducking inside the junior bathroom. I leaned against the back of the door, working to catch my breath. I wondered if Justin was still standing on the other side. I wondered if there was anything I could do to rattle him.

"Hey Tracy," I said, refixing a smile on my face when I saw the juniors in their shamanistic circle.

Tracy Lampert rose from her royal-blue beanbag chair in the corner of the bathroom. Her long black braids swung forward when she moved in to give me a hug. Usually, I'm the first to go off about how a girl could hardly step away to check her voicemail in Charleston without getting a hug on her return, but after my hallway tumble with Justin, I didn't mind a little bit of affection, even from the pseudo-psychic Lampert.

"You okay, Nat?" Tracy asked. Even though her signature sapphire-tinted glasses hid her eyes, it was almost like her voice was squinting at me. "Your energy orb is very present. Which can be a good thing or a bad thing, depending on—"

"I'm fine," I told Tracy.

She raised her eyebrows but dropped the subject.

"Sit down," she cooed. "Have some tea."

Tracy poured a steaming mug of chai from a hot pot on the windowsill, and her two cohorts Liza Arnold and Portia Stead sat down on the beanbag flanking her sides. Portia whipped her long hair up into a massive blonde bun, and Liza closed her eyes meditatively. I stifled a laugh, thinking that by the time these girls were seniors, they'd be so over this phase that they'd look back and laugh at themselves. But for now, I was in their court, so I just plopped down among them on the final beanbag in the ring.

"So," Tracy said, giving strange weight to the word. "How's life?"

I cocked my head. "Life's good," I said. "But why don't we talk about why you called me in here?"

Liza opened her eyes, coming out of meditation. She glanced at her watch, then at Tracy. "Just tell her. The bell's about to ring."

I lifted my chin. "Tell me what?"

"Okay, I'll just cut to the chase," Tracy said. Her voice changed and let in a rare hint of her natural southern twang, which made the bindi between her eyes look halfway ridiculous. "My sister-in-law is one of the ballot counters for the Ball this year," she said. "She told me this thing about Justin Balmer last night. Now I know you guys have a history—"

I held up a hand. "We *don't* have a history—"

"Whatever," Tracy said. "It's obvious you and Mike are really happy; I'm just saying that I thought you should know there's buzz about J.B. this year."

I could feel the blood rising to my face. Even though Palmetto Court was technically a student-driven vote, everyone knew that behind the scenes, the righteous right-wing school board kept a hawk eye on the ballot boxes to ensure that no one "unsavory" ended up with the crown.

I should have known J.B. would do something to secure a leg up with the ballot counters. What had he done? Bribed the judges? Not that I hadn't thought about it myself . . .

"Okay, which wrinkly ballot counter is that asshole screwing?" I blurted.

The juniors gasped, and Tracy covered her mouth to stifle a laugh. "No, sweetie, you misunderstood. The judges aren't exactly buzzing about J.B. in a good way." She tucked a braid behind her ear. "Between you and me, someone's trying to keep him off the Court. Some bad blood from last summer—I don't know the details. I was just telling you because—"

I could breathe again. I almost wanted to kiss Tracy.

"Because you knew I was worried about Mike," I said finishing her sentence.

"Exactly," Tracy nodded. "Nothing's certain, of course, but I figured I owed it to you to pass along the word. Your poker face isn't half bad. Still, I hate to see a pretty girl give herself premature worry lines when I can do something to help."

"Does Justin know someone has it in for him?" I asked, trying to smooth out my forehead without looking too obvious.

But before Tracy could answer, an apocalyptic crash of thunder boomed outside. All the girls crowded around the window to get a look.

"Oh my God!" Liza cried, gazing out at what was quickly turning into a full-fledged hailstorm. "We left the banners in the parking lot. They're tempera paint! They'll melt!"

Instantly, the junior bathroom mobilized. I guess hippies

couldn't always be at peace with the weather. All the girls started scrambling to get their massage oil back in their hemp bags so they could save their junior-spirit banners from the elements.

On her way out the door, Tracy cupped my elbow.

"J.B. doesn't know a thing," she said. "Probably best if we keep it that way—know what I mean?"

Then she and her friends scattered, taking their tempest outside. The only sign of life in the empty bathroom was the swinging door that led out to the hallway—the swinging door with J.B.'s face plastered on it.

Can't a guy change?

The question still rang in my ears. But I'd heard that one too many times before. So I stood before the half-ripped poster and ran my hand over his face, the way they do in the movies to close the eyes of the dead.

Then, glancing around the empty hallway, I snatched it off the door, folded it neatly in half, and dropped it in the junior-class recycling bin. I wasn't so far away from my own junior year that I'd forgotten how to voodoo.

CHAPTER *Two*

THE VALOR OF MY TONGUE

"I have had the foulest day," I said that evening, slipping my purple backpack off my shoulder and tossing it on the French window seat in Mike's bedroom.

He was standing in the doorway, wringing out of his rain-soaked football jersey, but when I started skivvying out of my damp jeans—just slowly enough to give him a little show—I could see his reflection in the window perk right up to attention.

"Define *foulest*," he said, taking a step toward me. The room was dark except for the warm glow of his bedside lamp and the diffused white light coming through the window from the golf club down below. Mike ran the back of his hand up the length of my leg and gave me a sexy half smile.

"Food-poisoning-from-Waffle-House foul, or just slightly more dire than yesterday's *foulest* day ever?"

"You're mocking me," I moaned, pulling away to face the manicured green of the thirteenth hole and the lush rolling tree line beyond the course. Clots of greenish clouds churned overhead, ready to turn to rain again any second.

"You're too clothed to be taken seriously," Mike said, pulling my attention back indoors and my body back to his. He tugged at the tight black turtleneck I was still wearing. "Aren't you the one who suggested the rule?" he teased, kissing my neck between each word. "Total. Naked. Honesty?"

I rolled my eyes but grinned as I pulled my shirt over my head. The room was cool, and I felt the prick of goose bumps rise along my arms. I stretched out diagonally across the king-size waterbed in my lucky black-bra-and-underwear set, then rolled over onto my stomach so Mike would have to climb on top of me to find a spot.

"Honesty later," I said, gesturing at my neck. "Kneading now. I've got a knot the size of Georgia right . . . yes, *there.*"

Mike had stripped down to his tartan boxers and assumed the masseur position over me. I let myself close my eyes and really breathe for the first time all day.

After finding out from Tracy how close we were to certain victory, I'd fidgeted through the rest of my classes, getting more and more anxious to plot something to ensure our win. By now, it was all I could think about. But there was something about Mike's hands on my neck, how powerful and strong they were. They made me let everything go.

I remembered the first time I'd seen his hands—strong, tan, gripping a baseball bat, definitely a force to be reckoned with. Since Mike's bedroom overlooked the ritzy Scot's Glen golf club, where kids from the other side of town—the wrong side of town—got their kicks by sneaking onto the course to chuck golf balls at the mansions. Totally adolescent, yes, but it's not like there was much to entertain a trailer-park kid on the Cawdor side of the bridge. It was part of the fun that the rich kids kept arsenals by their back doors to chase off the vandalizing have-nots.

Sure, I'd had a few good times with exactly those wrong kinds of guys, always in and out of juvie, often with names like Junior Junior. My old friend Sarah Lutsky used to say nothing heated up a redneck romance like a run-in with the law. But right around the time I met Mike, I'd decided to turn over a new leaf.

It was September fifteenth, freshman year, and I had just transferred over to Palmetto. My mom had recently remarried, *again,* finally accomplishing her life goal of moving us over to the right side of the bridge—and into the Palmetto school district. So when my golf ball sliced through Mike's bedroom window, it was—for a change—completely accidental. Not to mention the end of my very short golf career.

It's crazy to think about it now, but I'll never forget how, when Mike came out of the house swinging his baseball bat, wearing only a pair of crisp khaki shorts, my first instinct was to run. Sarah's take on getting caught had always been, "When the going gets rough, swim home."

"Hey, wait," Mike had called out, jogging after me. "Hang on, I thought you were . . . someone else."

I froze, standing by his pool in my brand-new golf polo and pleated white miniskirt—a gift from my new stepdad and the most expensive thing I'd ever owned. Right then I realized, for the first time in my life, that I had a right to be there. All I had to do was choose to own it.

Mike still didn't know exactly how influential that first meeting was. He liked to think our little make-out session by his pool shack was what made me remember the day so fondly and insist upon celebrating its anniversary every month. But we've been going strong for more than three years now (way longer than my mom's third marriage lasted). At this point, I figured, when it came to certain parts of my past, the whole "total naked honesty" thing only really needed to go so far.

As Mike went to town on my neck, I felt myself sinking

deeper and deeper into relaxation mode and let out a contented sigh.

"Hey, I know that sound," Mike leaned into my ear to whisper. "You're falling asleep. Don't forget you're not the only one in the world who needs a little after-school stress relief."

My eyes shot open, and I sat up on the waterbed, causing it to jiggle.

"Do you mean you're worried about Palmetto, too?" I said quickly. "I thought it was just me, but you must have seen all the posters today, too. Do you think we put enough up? Do you think we look better than everyone else?"

"Way to kill the mood," Mike joked. He rubbed his hand down my side. "I just meant I could use some . . . ahem . . . general stress relief . . . hint hint."

"Oh," I said, reaching over the edge of the bed for my bag to pop a piece of Juicy Fruit in my mouth. "That."

"Yeah," he said. "*That*. Don't sound too excited."

When I met Mike's eyes, I realized how stupid I'd sounded. I didn't even mean it. Being this close to his body always made me want to rip his clothes off. It wasn't that I'd lost sight of that; I just had the Ball on my brain.

"I'm sorry, baby," I said, burying my face in his chest. "That's not what I meant. You know I can't get enough of you." I started kissing my way down his stomach, which always left him paralyzed. I hovered right above his boxers to look him in the eye. "It's only that I want the whole school to want you just as badly . . . serving as their Prince."

He moaned and stroked my head. "I'll settle for *your* endorsement."

I ran my thumbs inside the waist of his boxers and clicked my tongue. "Uh-uh, that's not enough. You know I want to celebrate our status . . . with crowns."

"Why?" he whispered. "What status? Who cares about anything besides you and me?" He tried to pull me up to him, and I could feel our bodies fitting into their natural groove. I had to will myself to pull away.

"*I* care."

"Nat," Mike sighed. He sat back up and combed his fingers through my hair. "I know you've been fantasizing about the two of us getting crowned at the Ball for, like, our entire relationship, but you do know there is life after Palmetto Court, right?"

Mike was smirking at me the way that he did when I started to get carried away. His deep-brown eyes got all crinkled up, and his dark wavy hair flopped over his forehead. I'd have to remind Binky, his housekeeper, that his hair was about three, no, more than four days away from needing a trim—though it looked pretty cute for now.

Still, cute wasn't going to win us anything at this stage in our lives. Why was I the only one in the room who seemed to be aware of it? It was times like these when I realized Mike had no concept of what it meant to work for something. It was almost like, if he didn't already own it, or couldn't buy it with his charm, he had no use for it. Sometimes I wondered whether he was even capable of *wanting* something that was hard to get.

Now he leaned in for a kiss, but I held him back, pushing on his chest with two fingers. He was inches away from my mouth.

"I will die if Justin Balmer walks away with your crown," I said.

Mike sighed, collapsing back on the bed.

"I'm not getting into J.B. with you again," he said. He stared up at the glow of the solar-system stickers we'd stuck on his ceiling back when we'd first gotten together, back when Palmetto Court dreams seemed as far away as the stars outside.

"I can't believe how little you care about how much I care about this." I banged my fist down on the bed, making more waves. Then I quickly shoved it into my other hand to keep myself still. "Have you even *ordered* my Jessamine yet?"

Note: In case you're reading this from another planet, the Jessamine is not just the South Carolina state flower; it's also the longtime corsage of choice for Palmetto High School dances. Of course, somewhere along the line, the tacky southern flair for design infiltrated that tradition, and today's Jessamine is like a nouveau riche distant cousin of its former self.

In the old days, guys just picked fistfuls of the golden wildflower and pinned them to a brooch. But today's Jessamine can only be ordered from the Duke of Jessamines, and all the flowers look like they're on steroids. They're silk, about the size of a Frisbee, and decorated with all the bells and whistles (and ribbons and stickers and photo buttons and school spirit emblems—and I swear I saw one last year that lit up and played music) that your date can afford.

Guys custom-order them weeks in advance, and girls sport their Jessamines to school on the day before the dance. It's the only time of year you'll see cheerleaders in overalls—the denim bib holds up the weight the best. Jessamine Day has gotten to be so huge that if you're unlucky enough not to get asked to the Ball, you basically call in sick. It's better to flake than to show up flowerless.

I know it sounds intense. The Duke of Jessamines even has to hire a team of seasonal employees to help him make the corsages this time every year. Which is how my mother got her current job—and her current benefactor . . . I mean, boyfriend.

"Nat?" Mike brushed his thumb on my cheekbone, interrupting my thoughts. "I said I was going to order it tomorrow."

"MIKE!" I jumped up in horror. Picking out the right

Jessamine was the biggest, most public display of commitment a guy could make toward his girlfriend. "The dance is a week away! You know they run out of the best flowers."

Mike wrapped his leg around me. He tried again for a kiss, but I sucked in and pursed my lips.

"Have I ever let you down?" he asked.

I crossed my arms, and I couldn't decide whether I was fake-pouting or real-pouting. "Not yet," I responded.

"I never will," he said.

"I'll believe that when you beat J.B. for Prince."

Mike rolled his eyes and grinned. "Your one-track mind is very sexy. But I've told you, Balmer's cool now. He was just showing me his costume for the party this weekend."

Oh my God, in all the excitement, I'd completely forgotten about Rex Freeman's infamous Mardi Gras soiree.

It was the one time a year when every kid at Palmetto, save a few of the most self-righteous youth groupers, cut loose and got a little crazy. All the typical girls would be wearing feathered masks and fishnets, but I was determined to come up with something that stood out in the crowd of wannabe sluts. The boys would be all Panama hats, flasks in their jackets, and barely buttoned French-cut shirts. Often, they ended up looking more scandalous than the girls.

I did love to pick out costumes for us to wear every year, but I think my favorite part of Mardi Gras was seeing everyone all showered and appropriate at church the next morning, when you'd still be picturing them flashing for beads. It was something I looked forward to every year, but today, the thought of Rex's party was just one more thing getting under my skin.

"So what?" I asked Mike huffily. "You and J.B. were swapping beads in the locker room?" Mike and I had already agreed to keep our costume concept this year a surprise until we showed up at the party.

"Course not," Mike shrugged. "Just his. Dude's gonna wear a feather boa. It's hilarious."

"I doubt it," I said. The mental image of J.B. stumbling around drunk in a hot-pink feather boa did nothing for me— unless that feather boa could be used to publicly humiliate/ annihilate him.

Then Mike put his thumb on my lip. "Hey," he said softly. "If I promise to get you the Jessamine to shame all other Jessamines, will you kiss me already?"

I leaned into him and tried to gauge the look in his eyes. He looked totally earnest. I wondered if that would change if I clued him in on a few unsavory details about J.B. That would involve divulging some information about my past that I'd banished to the recesses of my mind, but you know what they say about desperate times.

"Come on," he coaxed again. "Kiss me."

I pulled Mike to me so that our lips just barely brushed when I spoke. "If I kiss you, will you promise to keep your costume plans a secret from J.B. until Saturday night?"

Mike's brow furrowed the way it did when he couldn't quite keep up with my logic but trusted me enough not to question it. His strong hands folded around me, and he pressed his lips to mine. His tongue parted my mouth, and when I opened up to him, I could feel a new kind of power moving in.

CHAPTER *Three*

THE BEST OF THE CUTTHROATS

When you're dating southern royalty, always pack a change of clothes.

There's the daytime getup (string bikini and gauzy black cover-up) that you bring to your boyfriend's bayside villa for the after-dinner jaunt on his state-of-the-art cigarette boat . . . and then there's the lavender-jersey tennis dress and impeccably white cardigan that you threw in your bag in case his blue-blood parents pop by the house unexpectedly for dinner . . . again.

"Look who's in the neighborhood!" Diana King trilled as she stepped into the foyer of the King family's weekend house. I listened for the *thwunk* of her alligator-skin duffel landing on the Persian rug in the middle of the massive foyer. Then I heard the rapid-fire clicking of her stilettos on the opalescent marble as she beelined up the stairs toward her youngest son's boudoir door, on which she patently refused to knock.

"That's my cue," I groaned, rolling off of Mike on the navy quilted bedspread. It was a sure bet that she'd be up here sniffing around before Mike could even collect himself after all the hard work I'd been doing.

"To be continued," Mike said, pulling on my earlobe with his lips. "Hi, Mom," he called loudly, crossing the room to rifle through his nautical mahogany trunk for some clothes.

I managed to shut my scantily clad self inside Mike's Jacuzzi-equipped bathroom exactly one nanosecond before Diana took over the bedroom. I could smell her signature Shalimar perfume as she stood in the doorway. And from the hurried rummaging in the next room, it sounded like Mike was still scrambling into his shirt. Perfect. As if Diana needed more ammunition to play Ice Queen with me.

"I didn't realize you were coming out today," Mike said smoothly, probably standing to give her the double-cheeked kiss she always insisted on. "What's the occasion?"

"'Tsk tsk," I heard Diana say, recalling my own mother's favorite zinger about that annoying blue-blood habit of speaking in onomatopoeias: *like they're not rich enough to buy a vowel?*

"Darling, don't act so surprised," Mike's mother was saying. "You can't think Natalie's the *only* one who likes to make use of our villa. She's here with you, no doubt?"

Sniff sniff. I envisioned her rhinoplastied—excuse me—deviated-septum-altered nostrils flaring with thinly veiled suspicion.

"She's, uh, in the shower," Mike covered for me, and I promptly turned on the faucet. I hadn't been planning on showering until *after* we finished what we'd started in the bedroom *and squeezed* in a couple hours of sunset tubing on the boat. But then again, whenever Mike's mother made a cameo, it wasn't unusual for our plans to go to hell in one of her designer handbags.

Huffily, I resigned myself to shampooing my hair. Minutes later, when I felt the waft of cold air from the shower curtain being pulled back, I jumped.

"Jesus," I gasped. "I thought you were—"

"My mother, coming in to soap your back?" He raised an eyebrow.

"Get in here." I grabbed his arm to pull him in. Finally, things were getting back to the way they belonged: steamy.

But Mike looked around, as if his family could see us alone in the bathroom.

"I can't," he said. "I have to help my parents unload the car. Mom was hoping we could all have dinner."

"Dinner?" I said. Dinner chez Diana's was so not part of the plan. I needed alone time with Mike to gear up for our big week. "What about the lake?"

Mike took the loofah out of my hand, turned my body around with one deft movement of his wrist, and started lathering my shoulder.

"Don't change the subject," I moaned.

"We can't exactly get out of it," Mike said. "I'll take you out in the boat after dinner."

I whipped my head around. "Just the two of us?"

"On a school night," he winked.

"Ooh," I smiled. "What will Mother think?"

Clean enough and appropriately attired in the tennis dress Mike had even laid out for me on the bed—what, did he think I was going to wear the teddy to dinner?—I tromped down the hardwood stairs.

Through the French windows, I could see Mr. and Mrs. King relaxing on the terrace facing the glittering water at the west end of the Cove. Diana was cross-legged in her navy-blue skirt suit, reading the paper and sipping her token glass of Viognier. Her frosted hair was gathered in a low bun at her neck and, as ever, her foundation was flawless. Mike's father, Phillip, who carried visible stress in every part of his body—and who Mike took after in looks alone—had his brow furrowed and was shouting into his cell phone. The toe of his polished leather dress shoe was making rushed circles in the air.

Nothing indicated the imminent parental dinner party. But

when I heard the telltale clamoring of pots behind the closed doors of the kitchen, I got it. Just because no King had set foot in that kitchen since they approved the architect's floor plan, it didn't mean someone else wasn't whipping up a feast in their honor. Of course, they couldn't travel the thirty miles to the shore without "help." Of course, they would have brought their housekeeper Binky in tow.

Binky and I had a complicated relationship—there were times, like right now, when I almost related more to her than to the rest of Mike's family. I knew that when she wasn't boarding with the Kings, she lived in my old neck of the woods, in Cawdor across the bridge. In fact, the first time I met Binky, we bonded over a shared love for the huevos rancheros at Dos Hermanos, a hole-in-the-wall Mexican joint near her house. It wasn't until Mrs. King cocked her head at me and asked when on earth I would ever have been on that side of town that I remembered my new position over here. I had to resort to stammering something I'm not proud of about getting really lost one time during my driver's ed test. After that, I learned to be cautious about what I let slip in front of Binky. By now, I knew this was easier to do if I just didn't blur the line between servant and the served.

"There you are," Mike said, coming in from the library. He kissed my forehead, all PG and appropriate. "I hope you don't mind, when Mom saw your dress, she asked Binky to iron it."

"Your mother went through my things?" I asked. So Diana, not Mike, had laid out my dress. I didn't think I had anything suspicious in my bag, but giving Diana free rein over my things was definitely not a precedent I wanted to set.

"We were just trying to help you do a quick costume change," Mike said, always the mitigator. "Speaking of costumes, are you going to give me a late-night preview of your costume for tomorrow?"

The Mardi Gras party. I'd finally settled on a costume, and after a tiny battle with Mike—why did guys always *want* to wear makeup and stockings?—I'd convinced him that this year, we were going to shock everyone by taking the classy route. It was a given that every one of my friends would still be rocking that tired brothel-employee look, and I loved the idea of being the only lady in the house. Mike's debonair get up this year was of equal importance. He was really going to stand out—especially next to Justin Balmer in a minidress.

"Our costumes for tomorrow are still a surprise, right?" I said to Mike. "You haven't told J.B. or anyone? This is our moment to outshine them—show we're really royalty material."

"Trust me," Mike said, taking my hand to go greet his royal family outside. "We'll blow the whole party away."

"Hello, Natalie." Mr. King stood up to give me a very charged squeeze on the shoulder. "Aren't you tan?" he asked, taking me in head to toe.

"Goodness," Diana said, peering at me over her paper. "She certainly is brown, isn't she?"

"Golf lessons," I piped up, lest either of them assume I'd been working in the field. "At the club."

Diana looked down at her own arms. "I'm so pale, like Scarlett O'Hara. You know that used to be the fashion." She looked around and gave us all a tight-lipped smile. "Who wants to take dinner on the terrace tonight?"

With a shrug, Mike deferred to me.

"Of course," I said, taking a seat on the patio between his parents. Like Mom always said: It doesn't matter where you are; if you act at home, you will be. Then again, I wasn't sure Mom's limited Emily Post library book repertoire would have gotten her far with this crowd.

Especially with someone like Diana, who picked up a silver bell from the glass tabletop and jangled her thin, Scarlett O'Hara-pale wrist. The high, tinny sound rang out across the yard, and I thought about what this unspoken summons might sound like to anyone out on the bay. Then again, the houses in the Cove (a.k.a. the Coveted) were so spread out, the Kings and I might be the only ones around for miles.

Seconds later, Binky arrived to answer her summons. She wore a starched black uniform that smelled of lavender, and the laces on her sensible black shoes were double-knotted. Her short dark hair had the telltale bluish tint of drugstore dye.

Her smile looked slack when she stood expectantly before the Kings.

"Our guest would like to dine outside," Diana said. "I hope that's not too much trouble for you."

"Of course not," Binky nodded. She looked at me. "Hello, Miss Natalie."

I smiled and nodded back at Binky but decided to keep my mouth shut. It was only the hundredth time I'd had dinner with Mike's parents, but I was still forever designated as the "guest."

It was getting to be that time of year in Charleston when it was still warm enough to swim, and the advancing sunsets always came as a surprise. The canopy of pine trees above us cast an acid-green tint on the Kings and me as each of us waited for someone else to pick up the conversation. Cicadas buzzed in the dusk. A pinecone thumped to the ground.

At the sound of voices near the dock, Diana beamed and rose from her chair. She gave her staid, ex-beauty-queen wrist twist to Mike's brother Phillip Jr. and his new fiancée, Isabelle, as they came up the path.

I noticed a sailboat docked in the King marina, but from the freshly pressed look of Phillip and Isabelle's matching white dinner clothes, I was guessing that they, too, had a couple of hired hands on deck.

"You made it," Diana called.

Isabelle doled out a slew of squeaky air kisses while Phillip Jr. moved in at the bar. "We heard your little dinner bell and just came running," he said dryly, dropping bitters into a bourbon.

Despite his namesake, Phillip Jr. had opted out of the family radiology business when he graduated from med school last year. Instead, he'd started his own practice and had since become one of Charleston's hottest young plastic surgeons. It was all very hush-hush—plastics being borderline unacceptable in a family of "real" doctors—but from the seamless skin around Diana's eyes when she smiled at her future daughter-in-law, it was obvious that someone had discovered the perks of having a son with an endless supply of botox.

"Isabelle, darling, I was just telling Natalie about the refurbishments you and Phillip are making to the boat," Diana lied, smoothing her future daughter-in-law's blonde tresses, which looked remarkably like her own.

She turned to me. "I'd ask you to join us after dinner for a cruise, but," she hesitated, searching for just the right words, "you seem to prefer a faster ride."

The daggers were out early tonight; we were barely into aperitifs. How to quip back that I'd sooner send myself down with the anchor before I spent another three hours droning on some sailboat with the Kings?

Mike had promised me a private moonlit ride on the

cigarette boat. But when I looked at him, miming his golf stroke across the lawn at his father's command, I knew our little boat cruise would dissolve instantly if he caught wind of a ride in Phillip Jr.'s boat. Mike hated being left out of family plans. Classic younger-child complex.

"We'd love to join you," I said. "It's just, I haven't been able to bring myself aboard a sailboat in years—not since what happened to Daddy." I held Diana's gaze. "I'm sure Mike told you about the accident?"

"Of course," Diana said evenly. She tilted her head slightly before turning to Isabelle. "Well, I'm sure the rest of us will still have an enchanting ride," she said, patting her protégé's acrylic-manicured hand. "Oh, there's Binky to refresh the drinks, thank God."

When the rest of the family descended on the silver cocktail platter, I found Mike and tugged on his sleeve.

"She still speaks to me like I'm disposable," I said through gritted teeth.

Mike looped his arm around my waist and squeezed my side. For one too-short second, the rest of them disappeared.

"It's not personal, Nat; it's tradition." His tone indicated that this was something I already knew. "Mom barely acknowledged Isabelle until Phillip put a ring on her finger. And our families have been friends for generations."

There it was. Even when Mike was trying to console me,

it was impossible not to address the ever-present hierarchy of Charleston breeding. What was it going to take to get the Kings to think I was worth a spot in their court?

"Just so you know," I said quickly as Binky wheeled out a tray of salads, "I declined your mother's offer to take a ride on P.J.'s sailboat after dinner." Before Mike could register a complaint, I added, "You know they make me nervous."

"I do?" Mike looked confused.

The ringing sound of the bell interrupted us.

"Dinner is served," Binky announced, and the whole happy family took a seat. I smirked when I noted that my place card had Mike seated directly across from me. I highly doubted Diana would have ordained this arrangement if she had any idea what my foot was reaching for surreptitiously under the table. Who likes a fast ride now, Mrs. King?

"So, Mikie," Phillip Jr. said, using the nickname I hated as he buttered a sweet potato biscuit. "Justin Balmer's old lady came in for a consultation today."

Have I mentioned what an infamous bore Phillip Jr. usually was? But suddenly he had my undivided attention.

"From the way she was talking," he continued, "the bags under her eyes aren't the only things sinking around Palmetto. How are your numbers in the projections for Prince? Is Mrs. Balmer full of hot air, or is J.B. actually going to give you a run?"

Diana dropped her fork to her plate in alarm. Her eyes shot up at Mike.

"Phillip's joking, Mother," Mike said, shrugging it off.

"Not really," Phillip quipped. He looked at his parents. "Remind me how many generations of Kings have been crowned at Palmetto? Four, or is it five?"

"It's *every* generation since the school has been in operation," Phillip Sr. said, motioning Binky to clear his plate. He raised his steak knife in Mike's direction so that it looked like an extension of his body. "This is not some little beauty pageant to be made light of, Michael. You know our family has a perfect record."

I'd always imagined that Mike was so nonchalant about Prince because it was the kind of thing his family might dismiss. But now I finally understood one of the many silent power struggles I waged with Diana: Every day after school, when I moved Mike's framed National Merit Scholars certificate to the front of his desk, someone replaced it with his football trophy after I went home.

So success was formulaic to the Kings. If adulthood was for serious, professional accomplishments . . . was it possible that high school, in their eyes, meant sports and popularity, to the point where they even trumped academics? So the Kings cared as much about Palmetto Court as I did. Suddenly, this little dinner party went from buzz kill to extremely beneficial.

"Of course, who can forget Phillip Jr.'s flawless coronation speech?" Diana recalled, dotting her mouth with a napkin. "What was it again, dear? 'As gratitude for this bestowed honor—'"

"'I will earn your absolute trust,'" Phillip Jr. finished, smugly nodding his head. I rolled my eyes at Mike to indicate that he would not be bringing that gem back to life at our coronation.

Phillip Jr. lowered his voice and cocked his head away from his mother. "Of course, if you ask Isabelle, it wasn't my *verbal* prowess she remembers about that day," he muttered, giving Mike a nudge. "Don't come a knockin' when you see a carriage rockin'—know what I mean?"

He and Mike shared a rare brotherly snicker at the reference to what went on behind closed carriage doors during the Prince and Princess's famously racy ride to the coronation. It was one of Palmetto's oldest traditions and also one of its most taboo. A half hour before the coronation ceremony, a horse-drawn carriage made two stops at the Scot's Glen country club. First to pick up the Prince in the Club Room, then to pick up the Princess outside the Ladies Lounge. The nearly crowned then took a ride around all eighteen holes of the golf course and were delivered for their grand entrance to the ceremony, just in time to make their speeches.

Depending on the relationship between the future royalties,

the carriage could either be a vaguely awkward or a totally hot ride. And, of course, it was always choice pickings for the rumor mill at school. If there was any chemistry at all between the Prince and Princess, sending a Princess into the carriage was much like sending a bride off to her marital bed. Hence Phillip Jr.'s bawdy boast, and hence Isabelle's icy not-in-front-of-your-folks glare.

"What about you, Natalie?" she asked, steering the conversation back toward more appropriate ground. "Are you on the Court for Princess, too?"

Before I could open my mouth, Diana snapped, "Don't change the subject, Isabelle."

I used my toe to nudge Mike's groin. When his head shot up and his eyes met mine, I raised my eyebrows in the most seductively threatening way I could manage at the dinner table. *Prime time to step up to the plate, love.*

"No one's changing the subject," Mike piped in obediently. "If I win anything, it'll be because of Nat."

Diana was banging the prongs of her fork on her dinner plate without realizing the entire table was trembling to the beat of her nerves. I popped another bite of filet mignon in my mouth, enjoying every delicious moment.

I had never seen Diana King so unglued. There was something gorgeously transparent about her poker face:

Had she been slacking in her duties as a high society mother?

43

Was there someone she needed to talk to?

Was it . . . gasp . . . too late?

"Really, Mr. and Mrs. King," I said sweetly, laying a hand on Diana's arm to silence the fork. "Don't worry about a thing." I wedged my toe further between Mike's legs, wondering briefly what accolades I could get for working open his fly using only my toes.

"Slightly easier said than done, dear," Diana said to me.

"I promise," I said, giving weight to each word. "I think your son and I have found a surefire way in." I glanced at Mike, unbuttoning him right there in front of his very buttoned-up family. "Pretty soon . . . we'll have this thing nailed."

Mike bit his lip. Sometimes it was hard to tell whether he was flushed from being turned on or whether he was embarrassed by a little innocent bon mot in front of his family. Everyone but me seemed relieved for the interruption when Binky brought out the palate cleanser.

"Thank you, Binky," Diana said, settling back into her role as Queen. "I think we'll ask you to serve dessert aboard P.J.'s sailboat. Of course, it will just be the four of us." She motioned to everyone but Mike and me.

Mike looked at me. "You're sure you don't want to—"

"Your mother and I already discussed it, remember? She was kind enough to consider my feelings after what happened to Daddy."

"Of course," Mike nodded, looking uncomfortable that he hadn't remembered instantly. Not that I blamed him—it wasn't exactly like I went around bragging about my dad's disappearance all the time. The tragic sailing accident was just a convenient story—clean enough for company and tragic enough that no one, including Mike, had ever really asked for particulars. "We'll just take the cigarette boat out then, Mother, if that's okay with you."

"Do as you wish," Diana said, standing up to excuse us from the table. "Just remember that when it comes to Prince next week, we're talking about more than just your wishes." She looked at me. "This is a family affair."

As Mike and I walked down the path toward the marina, he motioned me behind the pine tree where we'd once carved our initials. We stood pressed together in between the thick patches of green-mouthed Venus flytraps that grew like sunspots on the King's backyard. The plants' carnivorous jaws were open, waiting for their evening meal.

"You and my mom are sure in cahoots over my Palmetto Prince campaign," he teased. "Hey, I'm sorry about the sailboat thing. I should have realized."

"Over and done with," I said quickly. "And if being in cahoots with your mother gets you the crown, I guess I can suffer it for a week."

But I didn't feel in cahoots with Diana at all. In fact, my

pride was still stinging from her little "family affair" quip. Why didn't Mike seem to think anything of it? He was already busy untethering the boat. As I watched his arms flex while he worked, my whole body started buzzing. Really buzzing. Oh, wait—that was my phone buzzing in my purse.

I grimaced, thinking it was probably my mom, wanting me to pick up another bottle of wine for her on my way home. No mother has ever been so excited when her kid got her first fake ID.

But this text was no standard liquor-run call from Mom:

Guess who's back from the proverbial dead? I'm a free man again and want to celebrate with my favorite daughter. Could we meet for a drink?

The cool facade I'd managed all through dinner suddenly disappeared into the night. A thick black water moccasin slithered by my feet, and I gripped the wooden buttress of the marina for support.

"Nat?" Mike called from the boat. "The boat motor's running. Get down here so I can work on yours."

"Be right there," I said hoarsely.

Back from the dead indeed.

Dad.

CHAPTER *Four*

THRIFTLESS AMBITION

"Explain to me how it is that you're so calm," Kate asked me at brunch the next morning. We were seated along the palmetto-lined boardwalk of Catfish Row, finishing up our second round of cappuccinos on the patio of the famous MacLeer's Biscuit Café.

Anyone from Palmetto would tell you MacB's was the only place to brunch—not just for their buttermilk biscuits and homemade peach preserves, but also for the chance to scope out who showed up with whom. Since the rain clouds had finally given way to sun, the weather was in the high 60s, and it seemed like our entire school was trolling the historic wooden boardwalk outside MacB's.

At the round eight-top table closest to the cobblestone street, the student council kids—who never took a break—

struggled to make room for their bagels amid all their bulging Ball-planning binders. Near the water, Tracy Lampert and her junior-class coterie formed an amorphous cluster, swinging their bare feet over the boardwalk and tying dogwood blossoms in one another's hair. And at my usual table in the back corner of the patio, a crew of senior girls sat side by side in one long row, looking out at the ocean as they finished their egg-white quiches.

"Facials at five, Nat?" Jenny Inman asked as the girls filed past me toward the parking lot.

"I'll call you," I smiled, trying to assuage the hint of confusion as to why I hadn't filled in my usual MacB's seat next to her this morning.

The girls knew Kate was one of my favorite pet projects. This morning, I'd agreed to offer her a second opinion picking out a Mardi Gras costume from the thrift store down the street. But as I watched her simultaneously slurp up her cappuccino, check the tail of her long ponytail for split ends, and try to flag down our slip of a waitress for the bill, I wondered whether Kate needed help with more than just her costume. So much unnecessary multitasking—and Kate was usually really composed. When I realized she was still waiting for an answer to her question, I decided not to mention the fact that frantic people had a strangely mellowing effect on my mood.

"I'm calm," I suggested instead, "because I've already got

a costume for tonight. You're panicking," I said, taking in the throngs of Mardi Gras-crazed Palmetto kids all around us, "because you're just giving into the vibe."

Just then, a table of Bambies brushed past our table, wailing over the limited stock of size-one fishnets at the costume store around the corner.

"You're right," Kate met my eyes and laughed. She flipped her amber hair over her shoulder. "Screw the vibe!"

I offered her a stick of gum and cocked my head at the sea of departing Bambies. "I take it you're opting out of the sophomore-class costume this year?" I asked. "I heard something about . . . brothel-chic?"

Kate snorted, signing the credit-card slip the waitress had finally brought over. We stood up and pushed in our wicker chairs.

"Please," Kate said, "and become another Bambi blend-in?" She shuddered, making her long hair shimmer in the sun. "I'd rather join the church choir."

I grinned at the image of Kate on the pulpit with a bunch of youth-group kids and threw down a couple of extra dollars on the table before we left. Though my mother would never willingly admit it these days, she'd been a waitress the first fourteen years of my life, so I was well-versed in the injustices of under-tipping.

Kate looked around and lowered her voice to a husky

whisper. "Tonight is my night to seal the deal with Baxter—who *still* hasn't asked me to the Ball."

"*That's* why you're freaking out," I teased. Baxter Quinn was Palmetto's most legendary drunk and the dealer for most of our school's after parties. He was tall and light-haired and sexy in a lanky deadbeat sort of way. Even though he often couldn't hold himself upright, somehow he was never at a loss for girls.

"And that's why you're so calm," Kate said, tugging me over a series of puddles on the clapboard promenade—and out of the earshot of the rest of Palmetto. "You have the state's greatest built-in date. I bet you can't even remember what it's like to stress over a guy."

For just a second, my feet dragged on the boardwalk. Stressing over one guy in particular was exactly what I'd been trying *not* to do—ever since that unsettling text from my dad last night. Suffice it to say, Dad being "a free man again" was not exactly the good news he claimed it was.

Already, I could feel myself overexerting my jaw on the stick of gum I'd just unwrapped. Whenever the Juicy Fruit lost its flavor in less than five minutes, I knew I needed to find another way to chill out.

Kate stopped in front of a three-story southern-style bright-green row house with a wraparound purple-painted porch. A wooden sign swung on its hinges from the rafters overhead: *Weird Sister's Closet.*

Kate pulled open the stained-glass door and stepped inside. Like most of the mansion-turned-lingerie boutiques on Catfish Row, the Weird Sister's Closet was brimming with all things cleavage-enhancing. Posters of busty movie stars papered the walls, and strapless bras of all shapes and sizes filled the racks. But since it was on a cobblestone side street of the beaten path of the boardwalk strip, Kate had already assured me that the Weird Sister was the one place in Charleston's gentrified red-light district that would be Bambie-free today.

"What's with the puckered-up puss," Kate said, looking at me. "Where's your brink-of-royalty smile?"

Banishing thoughts of my father, at least for the time being, I conceded with a small, involuntary grin. Kate was right. Being on the brink of royalty was something to smile about, especially after all of our planning. In just a few days, fingers crossed, Mike and I would be happily crowned.

All the campaigning would be over, and the two of us could just bask in the success of our mutual hard work. We'd stay up late, editing our coronation speeches and practicing our waltz for the Ball. Yes, we had a waltz. And after the Ball, we'd pack a bottle of champagne, head straight for our spot at the secret waterfall near Mount Pleasant, and not come home until sunrise.

It'd be just the two of us, just like we'd always planned.

"That's what I'm talking about," Kate nodded, taking in the

change in my demeanor. "Now, let's address my main issue, which is *feathers on a spandex butt.*" She held up a red-sequined catsuit, flipping over the hanger to show off the tuft of red feathers right over the butt. "Do we love it or leave it?"

"Um, is that a tail?" I asked, half-appalled, half-intrigued.

"Just so you know," said the wild redheaded shop owner, clearing her throat behind the cash register, "we also have that in purple."

"Only certain women can wear purple." Kate grinned at me. "Like Nat." Then she clutched the red catsuit to her chest and gave me a devilish wink. "I think I'll take this baby for a test drive."

When she ducked into the dressing room, I laughed and shook my head. As the daughter of the wealthiest litigator in Charleston, Kate had a certain leg up on a lot of the other girls at Palmetto—the girls who just had "enough" money.

Kate's mother was certifiably insane (if those country club walls could talk), but because of her husband's untouchable bank balance, everyone called her "eccentric" instead of "crazy." Like there were just certain words that didn't apply to billionaires. So Kate, unlike most girls, could get away with piercing her tongue, adding a new tattoo to her arsenal every year . . . and wearing sequined, feathered spandex—all without ever risking being called a tramp. Maybe that was why I liked her: She lived like someone with no fear.

Having climbed up from the opposite end of the money spectrum, I ran my hand along a row of leather bustiers and felt renewed pride that my own costume was the opposite of everything in this store. I was just dipping into a fantasy of Mike and I, all dressed up and gliding through the party tonight, when someone stepped around the corner and held out the skanky catsuit in purple.

"Thought you might want to try this on," Justin Balmer purred.

The woodsy notes of his aftershave overtook me. And I thought nothing could out-stink the sensual jasmine aromatherapy candle that the Weird Sister was burning by the cash register. Eau de J.B. wasn't an empirically bad smell; maybe it was the proximity to him that turned my stomach.

I was trying not to look at the catsuit—or the way his blond hair fell over his eyes—so I focused on his sweatshirt. It was the same Palmetto varsity football sweatshirt that Mike lent me for the games.

"What do you say?" J.B asked, fingering the feathers on the back of the catsuit. A surprising shivery feeling spread through my chest.

"But you saw it first," I said coolly. "I couldn't deprive you of the perfect Mardi Gras costume."

"Who's said anything about a costume?" he said. "I just think this might accentuate some of your best features."

"You mean my growing boredom with your advances?" I said, sidling past him in the lingerie-cramped aisle.

J.B. put his hands on my shoulders, masseur-style, and breathed into my neck. "So what does the Princess have up her sleeve for tonight's costume?" he whispered.

I spun around. "That's for the Prince to know, and you to obsess over."

A frustrated grunt from Kate in the dressing room made both of us jump back. I'd completely forgotten she was still back there trying on the catsuit.

"How's it going?" I called into the curtain, praying she hadn't heard J.B.

"Bye-bye butt feathers," she called, sounding oblivious. "Anything else out there worth stuffing myself into for Baxter's benefit?"

J.B. raised an eyebrow at me. With a magician's flourish, he lifted the first thing in arm's reach off the rack and held it up for my approval. It was a gaudy hot-pink satin corset. If Kate wanted to catch Baxter's eye, this would probably do the trick.

J.B. flung the hanger over the door of the dressing room and, without thinking, I added, "Why don't you try this one?"

J.B. raised his fist at me, in recognition of our teamwork.

As if the two of us would actually fist bump over anything. I rejected him but still stood there, frozen to my spot.

After a pause, J.B. lowered his fist and sighed. A tuft of blond hair blew up from his forehead. The green lettering on the sweatshirt matched his eyes perfectly, so they stood out even more than usual, almost taunting me. I was torn between wanting to break his stare and not wanting to be the one to have to look away first.

"Stop looking at me like that," I whispered finally, hating that my voice sounded so small, that my breath felt so tight.

"It's just a smile, Nat," he said.

For a second, Justin Balmer sounded almost defensive. But then he licked his lips and bared his teeth at me. It sent a shiver down my spine.

"You know," he sneered, going back to being the animal I knew, "I find your doggedness to win this pageant a little, well, amusing." He leaned forward, dropped the purple cat suit in my arms. "And when I get amused," he continued, stepping past me, "it makes me want to play."

I squinted at J.B. standing in the doorframe, stroking his chin.

"Fine." I couldn't help grinning. "Game on."

"Who are you talking to?" Kate called from the dressing room just as J.B. stepped out onto the street.

"No one," I said quickly, turning around just in time to see Kate fling back the curtain. She shimmied out of the dressing room, wearing nothing but the pink silk getup, which fit her like a glove.

"You'd better be ready to throw down tonight," she sang, dancing up against me.

Catching a final glimpse of Justin walking toward the boardwalk, I crossed my arms and said, "Oh, I'm ready."

CHAPTER *Five*

CHARMED LIFE

"Welcome to Bourbon Street," Rex Freeman said, opening the door to his parents' Palmetto mansion Saturday night. He was topless, a jester hat covering his signature red buzz cut. He had on jean cutoffs and flip-flops. He was wearing so many strands of beads around his neck, you couldn't see his buff, freckle-covered upper body—which might have been a shame, but I knew that in his efforts to see the upper bodies of every ho in this room, Rex would have to give up most of those beads before the night was over.

He was grinning at the sea of Bambies separating Mike and me from the entrance to the party. "You ladies can hang your coats in the closet if I can hang these beads on your—"

"Excuse me," I said, pulling Mike's hand past the tittering

crowd of girls. "But before things get too fleshy in the foyer, you don't mind if we just squeeze through, do you?"

Mike shook his head and smirked at me.

"Sorry, man," he said, fist-bumping Rex on his way through the door. "You know Nat doesn't have much tolerance for Bambi hide."

"Pas de problem," Rex shrugged. "More for me."

I reached around Rex's neck for a strand of particularly garish beads. They were hollow metallic plastic and shaped like peacock feathers.

"Fancy," I said. "And ooh, they light up. Mind if I?..."

Rex grinned at Mike, the freckles on one cheek scrunching together. "You know, most girls would do anything to earn such special beads. Either I'm already sloshed or you have a very powerful girlfriend."

"Not that those two things are mutually exclusive," Mike joked.

Rex motioned for us both to lean in and nodded at a banner overhead, which read: *Lick'er in the front, pok'er in the rear.*

"Ignore the signs," he said. "Though there is poker out back. But you'll find the high-end booze upstairs in my dad's library." His face got serious. "I tell you this on a need-to-know basis."

"*Discreet* is our middle name," I said. "Thanks, Rex."

As Mike and I headed toward the need-to-know stash of

library liquor, we could hear Rex turn back to the scantily clad pubescents in the foyer.

"Now before I grant you beauties entrance to the party," he was saying, "I just need one small token to prove your undying Rexfection—"

Mike was shaking his head and laughing, but when I caught a glimpse of the two of us ascending the curved staircase, I stopped us both in our tracks.

"What's wrong?" Mike asked.

I pointed at our reflection in the massive gilded mirror spanning the wall. We'd been so rushed leaving my house for the party—so as to avoid Mom's wobbly camera-wielding hand—that this was my first full-length view of our ensemble.

My tastefully sequined soft-pink flapper dress was capped off by long white gloves and strappy silver kitten heels. Mom had spent an hour curling my dark hair into ringlets that fell a few inches below my shoulders. Every girl here would be likely sporting an over-sprayed updo, but Mike liked to be able to run his fingers through my long hair. Plus, I always felt more elegant with it down. The thick brown waves framed my minimally made-up face and the one gaudy indulgence I'd allowed myself for the party—fake eyelashes. I batted them demurely at Mike in his black top hat, tailored tux, and ruffled French-cut chemise, and in the mirror, he gave me a sexy wink.

Hand in hand, we looked like royalty. The perfect couple.

I still hadn't figured out how to respond to—or sufficiently avoid—my dad's disturbing text from the night before, but this glimpse of Mike and myself on the stairs was the first thing that had made me feel any better about the black cloud of problems past now hanging over my head.

Look at me. Look at us. I had come *too* far to get pulled back down.

"I'm so glad it was my idea to go classy this year," Mike joked.

He took the opalescent feather mask out of my hand and twirled it around on its stick before holding it up to my face.

"Yes, you're a real mastermind." I smirked, mounting the top stair and pushing open the curved wooden door to the library.

Inside the plush-carpeted room was your basic made-to-order rich folks' library. Floor-to-ceiling shelves showcased all the big classics of the western canon with their gold-embossed titles on thick, faded spines. Two maroon leather shrink's couches faced each other in the center, and a rolling ladder gave the whole place that extra touch of class. You got the feeling that the actual books were more of a backdrop to the library's main event, which was, of course, the crystal liquor cabinet near the windows.

It was a pleasant surprise to find that Mike and I were alone. Maybe Rex had been more discerning than I gave him credit for about who comprised the need-to-know set. While Mike uncorked a bottle of champagne, I stepped out onto the balcony for some air.

"What should we drink to this time?" he asked, coming up behind me with two brimming glasses.

I looked down at the yard below us where the party was in full swing. Rex had set up the same beaded canopy he used every year. And the same drunken silhouettes were clustering around the pool. There might have been something comforting in such familiarity, but tonight I just found it boring.

I looked at Mike and raised my glass. "To shaking things up."

"I have always wanted to shake things up with you on a balcony," he whispered. We kicked back our flutes of the primo champagne, and Mike swooped me up in his arms. He dipped me low, and his hand moved up my dress. I tipped my head back and moaned. The air was crisp and cool out on the balcony, but the heat emanating off of Mike made me feel lightheaded—or maybe that was the champagne's contribution. His hands felt so warm, so firm, so familiar, so—

"Lights, camera, *action*," a thick southern twang interrupted us. We looked up into the bright-white bulb of a video camera.

"Don't you know how to knock?" I asked, yanking my dress back down.

Baxter Quinn, dressed all in black, loomed over us with a camera perched on his shoulder. To add to my annoyance at being interrupted, I couldn't help frowning at the fact that Baxter was noticeably Kate-less. His light hair contrasted starkly with the creepy bags under his eyes. He was heroin-hot, and I could see why Kate would go for him, though he was miles from my taste. He looked like a vampire with that long coat of his flapping lightly in the breeze.

"Now how am I supposed to get the good stuff on tape if I knock?" he sneered. "Anyway, the last time I checked, this library was open to anyone Rex gave the green light to."

I raised my eyebrows and crossed my arms over my chest.

"The rich," Baxter said, gesturing at Mike. "The royal," he continued, turning to me. Finally, he pointed at himself. "And the relief." He opened up his black trench coat to expose a pharmacy's worth of powders and pills.

Mike nodded at Baxter's trench coat. "Are you so stoned you forgot it was a costume party?" he asked.

Baxter went to punch Mike's shoulder playfully, but instead he stumbled into the coffee table and ended up sprawled on the couch. Anyone else, I would have helped to his feet, but since Baxter's next stumbling fall would only be a matter of minutes away, I decided to save my energy.

"Don't you recognize my costume?" he slurred at Matt, making himself comfortable on the couch and crossing his legs on the coffee table. "Every dude knows that the best part of Mardi Gras is *Girls Gone Wild*. Since I dabble in filmmaking, I'm shouldering the task. All the top tits are out tonight."

I rolled my eyes, suddenly glad Kate wasn't here. "I didn't think Rex would give the library liquor green light to such a strung-out drunken pig."

"Feisty, Nat," Baxter said, leaning over and attempting to run a finger up my thigh from the couch. I swatted him off.

"Let's see that crotch shot again," he said. "Usually, things don't get that hot and heavy till at least midnight." He fiddled with the camera to play back some of his footage. "So far the juiciest thing I've got from down below is Justin Balmer tripping over his boa."

"What?" My ears perked up. "Let me see that. What's J.B. doing?"

"Asking to get punked is what he's doing," Baxter said, rewinding his footage to show us. "Someone should cut that kid off. He's one drink away from being worth the price of admission."

"You said it," I muttered as Mike and I leaned down to look over Baxter's shoulder. The camera was so wobbly that it was hard to see much, but J.B. was definitely making an ass of himself. He was poolside, flashing a sock-stuffed lacy bra he must have borrowed from some Bambi. He was sporting red lipstick and a short leather skirt with fishnets—pretty much the opposite of classy.

My eyes narrowed.

"Let's get down there," I said.

Mike nodded, happy for a reason to get away from Baxter. He made a last run for the good champagne.

"Royal road pop," he said, handing me the refill. "Who knows what the plebs are drinking down there?"

"You sure you don't want to do one more sex scene for the camera?" Baxter called out. "I could make you big on the Internet."

"Bye, Baxter," I said, leaving him slumped on the studded leather couch. "Thanks for the preview."

On the staircase, Mike and I paused again for another pose in front of the gilded mirror. Why was it that every time I caught a glimpse of myself looking so good, my father's trashy text flashed into my mind?

I started down the stairs again, but Mike pulled on my hand.

"Don't stray too far when we get down there," he said. "Can't have some masked man swooping in on you."

"Promise," I whispered back, glancing once more into his dark eyes.

In the kitchen, we passed the crawfish-boil buffet and the sign above it reading, *Bite the Tail and Suck the Head*. We paused behind a crowd of guys that had formed in front of the refrigerator. They each had a beer in one hand and a string of beads in the other. They were attempting a very drunken drum roll on their thighs.

"What do we have here?" Mike asked.

"Ask and you shall receive," one of the guys answered, tossing Mike a strand of beads.

Soon, a line of girls filed in to stand in a row before the crowd. Their hands were poised at the hems of their shirts.

"And . . . flash wave!" one of the guys cued.

The girls all whooped, and one by one, they lifted up their shirts in a contagion down the line. When all the lacy bras had been shown off, everyone was rewarded with exchanges of beads and saliva.

"Encore!" the guys shouted.

"Moving on," I said to Mike, and pulled him out to the tent.

At least the party outside was a step up on the classy scale. A band played old New Orleans blues songs on a rotating stage in the middle of the dance floor. Most of the upper-classmen were getting freaky around the band, holding giant feathered masks up to their faces.

From the bar, Kate waved in her hot-pink negligee. Her hair was in a high braided bun, and she seemed to be the only girl at the party who hadn't bothered to cover up her face with a mask. Her feathered heels clacked on the parquet as she dashed over to us.

"Don't you two look all regal?" she asked, giving Mike a once-over and me a solemn nod of admiration.

"We ran into Baxter upstairs," I said, watching her face light up as she tugged the negligee lower on her hips. I leaned in and cupped her ear. "He looks like he could use a little mouth-to-mouth resuscitation."

"Say no more," she purred, then pounced past us towards the house. I wasn't sure why she was after Baxter at all, but I was nothing if not charitable to the deserving. I wouldn't stand in their way. And anyway, I had more important things on my mind. Like finding J.B.

I scanned the rest of the crowd, spotting some senior girls in the far corner. They were serenading each other with massive multicolored boas. It was one big cloud of feathers flying over variations of tight black dresses.

"You want to go dance with the girls?" Mike asked.

I looked around to see what else was going on. I did love to dance, and there was something pretty sexy about everyone being incognito behind his or her mask. But I also wanted to be *cognito* when Mike ran into J.B.

An unwelcome hand on my ass told me I didn't have to wait any longer. I spun around and lowered my mask.

"Oh, I'm sorry," J.B. purred. "I thought you were someone else. A girl I used to know. My mistake."

I raised my palm to slap him, but Mike was standing right behind me.

"Hands off," I muttered to J.B.

"C'mon, doll face. Don't you know flesh is fair game on Mardi Gras?"

"Don't call me that," I hissed, my stomach seizing up at the sound of the nickname. "And for the record, my flesh is never fair game for you."

"Hey," Mike said, joining the conversation. "Balmer, you are one fugly woman."

"And you didn't dress the part," J.B. said, taking in Mike's tuxedo. From the self-conscious look on his face, it might finally have occurred to him how ridiculous he looked. "I thought you were going all out with me."

"Change of plans," I shrugged, thinking back to what Baxter had said upstairs about J.B. asking to get punked. "You look like you need another drink. Maybe it'll make you forget how unflattering those fishnets are." I turned around and spotted a crowd gathered next to the pool. "Look," I said innocently. "Keg stands. That looks fun."

"You want to do a keg stand?" Mike asked.

"No," I said. "J.B. does."

J.B. looked me up and down. His eyes were glassy and drunk. I couldn't figure out why I suddenly felt more naked than I had when Mike had my dress hiked up around my waist.

"Well, that sounds like a dare," he said.

Within minutes, Mike, Rex, and a couple of their JV football runners had J.B. lifted in the air. His legs were splayed out, and his mouth was poised over the keg to take it. I didn't even have to lift a finger to get the crowd to gather around.

"Chug! Chug! Chug! Chug!" the whole party cried out in unison.

J.B. spent a reputable amount of time sucking off the keg, and I sidled to the front to see his swollen face lurch with beer. When he made the mercy cut-off sign, the guys lifted him back up, then set him down. A cheer rang out across the party for the green-faced victor. I stood among my senior girls and waited for him to do something lewd enough to shock the crowd. Everyone knew Justin Balmer was no peach when he got trashed.

"Clear out," J.B. yelled, stumbling toward the bushes. "I'm gonna puke."

"Vile," my friend Amy Jane Johnson said, offering the senior girls swigs from her grandmother's old flask. "Keg stands are so bourgeois. Why is J.B. doing that?"

"That's not what you said when you made out with Dave Smith right after he did a keg stand last summer," Jenny

Inman teased her, tugging on her uncharacteristically short black shirt.

"That was different," Amy Jane said, fanning herself with her mask. "Dave Smith played at Wimbledon. He gets carte blanche."

"Encore," someone hollered at J.B. I looked up to see Baxter and Kate's silhouettes huddled together on the library balcony. "Boot and rally!" Baxter yelled.

Amazingly, J.B. answered the call to binge-drinking duty. Disgusted as my friends and I claimed to be, we cheered with just as much enthusiasm when the whole thing started up again.

After the guys had set J.B. shakily back on his feet, Rex got up on the microphone and clanked a fork to his crystal goblet.

"Okay, merry makers," he called. "As master of this party, I decree a skinny-dipping convention. In the pool. ASAP. You've got five minutes to get these heinous costumes off." He gestured at a junior guy's ripped gold-lamé tank top. "Find a dry place for your feathers, and get these gorgeous bodies in the water." For emphasis, he grabbed a Bambi's ass. "Rex's orders—or get the hell out."

Instantly, the whole mood of the party shifted as everyone flowed toward the pool. Seniors staked out lounge chairs for their clothes, while Bambies, who were virgins to Rex's party rules, squabbled over whether it was dark enough to feel okay about getting naked.

I felt Mike's hand take mine. "C'mere," he whispered.

"No way, I'm not skinny-dipping," I said quickly.

"Yes, I'm aware of your weird inexplicable aversion to skinny-dipping," he said, pulling me toward the bushes. "That's not what I had in mind."

I grabbed Mike's hand and smiled at him. He'd totally picked the right time for a private rendezvous in the side yard.

But when we got there, I was surprised to see J.B. slumped over against a dogwood tree. A cloak of Spanish moss hung down like a curtain separating us from the rest of the party.

"That second keg stand did him in," Mike said. He looked worried.

"So he let loose. What's the big deal?" I said. "He's a big boy; he can handle a little bit of—"

"Alcohol poisoning?" Mike finished.

I sighed. The pool party had gotten so loud, I could barely hear myself think. If everyone was already skinny-dipping, this soiree was playing out just like any other. If we stayed here, shaking things up might be a lost cause.

I squatted down in front of J.B. He was pretty catatonic.

"He probably just needs some air," I said finally. "Let's take a drive, just the three of us. Maybe we can bring him back to life."

CHAPTER *Six*

TOIL AND TROUBLE

"Ugh, he's total dead weight," I complained to Mike minutes later as we hauled J.B.'s limp body out to the driveway. "Why'd we park so far away?"

"I don't think we planned on this development," Mike said, looking unconcerned, like his end of the load was about as heavy as a feather boa.

He was holding J.B. under the armpits, and I had him by the legs. I was staggering under the weight, but that didn't stop me from enjoying a prime view of how green our patient looked around the gills.

Mike clicked the unlock button on his Tahoe. It was a good thing we'd brought his car tonight instead of the tiny, slightly used Miada that my mom's new beau had just bribed her with.

"Let's haul him in," Mike said.

We laid Justin across the backseat, and Mike rolled down the windows to let in some cool night air.

"I think I've got a water bottle in my football bag somewhere," he said, walking around to the trunk to rummage through his stuff.

Alone, more or less, with J.B. for a minute, I looked down at his face. He was going to feel like crap in the morning, but for now, he looked so peaceful. Even under all the makeup, you could see his fair skin and the freckles that gave him that deceiving boyish charm.

His red lipstick had faded to a brassy stain that crept out around the corners of his mouth, his eyelashes were clustered together by a pretty sad mascara job, and there was glitter, well, everywhere. Before I realized what I was doing, I ran my hand across his forehead to smooth out a gluey clump of the glitter from his eyebrow. I brushed a lock of blond hair back from his eyes.

They opened.

"Nat," he whispered. "Is that you?"

"Found it!" Mike called from the trunk of the car. He walked around and delivered an old Nalgene bottle with the Palmetto High School crest decaled in white. "Here," Mike said to J.B. "Drink this."

"I can't drink anything else," J.B. groaned. "I'll puke."

"Wouldn't be the first time tonight," I added, hoping to undermine whatever weird moment J.B. and I had just had.

"Where are we?" J.B. asked. He looked so helpless.

"Getting you away from that party," Mike said.

J.B. nodded, took a messy drink of water, and passed out again on the seat.

Mike chuckled and shut the door behind him. Then he leaned me up against it, stroked my hair, and pressed his body into mine. I could feel the familiar warmth spread through me, but I was thinking about what this would look like through the window if J.B. came to right now: my dark hair spread out against the glass, my arms pinned over my head, Mike's broad shoulders covering mine.

Mike kissed me, then looked into my eyes.

"Where to?" he asked.

"Just drive."

Mike started the car, and soon we were rolling out of Rex's long circular entryway, past what seemed like a never-ending row of our classmates' sports cars and jacked-up SUVs.

"Is it weird that *this* was our last Mardi Gras party?" I said, thinking about what was still going on at the pool. I didn't usually skip out on a social gathering until . . . well, until I was sure there was no more drama to be missed and gossiped about back at school the next week.

"What do you mean our last Mardi Gras party?" Mike asked. "What about next year? And the year after that? You know, I hear some people celebrate Mardi Gras *every* year."

"You know what I mean," I said, chipping off a flake of my pale-pink nail polish. Nervous habit. I could never keep a manicure longer than a day. "It's our last Palmetto High Mardi Gras. Our last Rex Freeman Mardi Gras. Next year, who knows where everyone will be. Things could be totally different." I ran my fingernails up the back of Mike's neck. "Don't you ever feel like this whole year is one long *last* time?"

Mike squeezed my thigh. "If Rex heard you talk like this, he'd throw another Mardi Gras party tomorrow. I promise, senior year at Palmetto does not mark the end of things." He looked in the rearview mirror. "Isn't that right Balmer? How you doing back there, Balmer?"

"Sick," J.B. groaned. "Very sick."

"Don't you dare throw up back there, Balmer," I turned around to threaten. "Here," I said to Mike. "Pull in up there and let's park."

"At the church?" Mike asked, looking nervous. Poor guy, he got weirded out enough having to be there once a week.

"Why not?" I shrugged. "It's not like the minister's doing drunk-driving patrol at one in the morning."

"I'm not going to church today, Mom," Justin moaned from the back. He was totally out of it.

"Did he say what I think he said?" Mike asked.

I started cracking up. I tried to imagine the tone of voice J.B.'s mother might take when she caught him doing something against her strangely lenient rules. Most of the week, Mrs. Balmer was probably too focused on counting the money in her boob-job piggy bank to give much thought to what her children did, but she always did drag her boys to church on Sundays. There was nothing more gauche than being seen at the pews without the arm candy you'd spawned.

"Well, Justin-honey," I said, channeling his mother's thick molasses drawl, "I think you got some sins that need atonin' for. What better place is there than the house of God?"

"Nat," Mike warned.

"I'm just screwing with him," I laughed. "Trust me, he won't remember any of this tomorrow."

Mike pulled into a spot near the chapel and turned off the car. We got out and opened the door to the backseat.

"Heave ho," Mike said, and we lifted J.B. up again and carried him to the lawn.

"Let's park him where they set up the nativity scene around Christmas," I said. "He'll look just like a little baby Jesus."

"No," J.B. whined, still sounding really loopy. "Mom, I can't go to church dressed like this. I look like Grandma with a hangover."

By then, Mike was laughing so hard he could hardly carry his end of the load, but I held onto J.B.'s fishnet-covered ankles and was struck by a brilliant beyond brilliant idea.

He was half-comatose and *still* totally consumed by the

thought of his reputation being on the line because of his slutty costume choice.

Now whose fault was that?

I looked at the lipstick, and the feather boa, and the one patent-leather high heel he still had on. And suddenly, I saw them all in a whole new light. Sunlight. It rose pretty early Sunday mornings in the Bible Belt. And everyone who was anyone went to church—including certain Palmetto Court ballot counters. Tracy *had* said some of them were already questioning J.B.'s candidacy for Prince. And Baxter *had* said J.B. was asking to get punked showing up at the party dressed in drag.

"Mike," I said slowly and quietly, "how funny would it be to leave him here?"

"Uh, not very," Mike said, finally done laughing.

"Think about it." I sank to the ground beside him and started running my fingers through his hair. "Perfect little Justin Balmer, exposed as a cross dresser?"

Mike looked unconvinced.

"Come on," I coaxed. "We haven't pulled one of our pranks in so long. He'll probably wake up when the pastor gets here first thing in the morning, anyway. He'll just have to hitch home in *those* clothes, that's all."

"But . . ." Mike started to protest as I kissed along his jawline. "Well, he does live all the way out in West Palmetto," he said.

"Exactly," I said, feeling the momentum build behind my

plan. "And do you really want to drive that far when you've been drinking?"

Mike shrugged and gave me the smallest twitch of a smile. I had him. I knew it.

"I guess it'd be sort of funny. As long as we leave him the water and make sure he has our numbers in his phone."

"Totally," I agreed. "We wouldn't want to take it too far." I looked over to make sure J.B. was still out. Check.

Back in the car, I grabbed the water bottle and reached into my bag for my lipstick. It wasn't quite as flashy as the color J.B. had been wearing earlier, but I figured it was the least I could do to freshen up his face before we ditched him.

The car was humming. Mike turned around from the driver's seat.

"Babe, I'm getting freaked out," he said. "Hanging out alone, drunk, at church. It's spooky. Hurry up, okay? I'll pull the car around."

"Sure." I nodded, all sympathetic girlfriend. "Be right back."

I was about to shut the door when something else caught my eye. It was a reel of the woven white rope that the Kings used to keep their boats tied up at the marina. Hmm, I didn't see why it couldn't be used to tie up *other* things. Even though Mike had agreed to this because he thought J.B. would wake up and run away before the first church bells rang, it might be funnier to give the kid just a little bit of a handicap. Everybody knew:

What goes around comes around, and it was long past J.B.'s turn to feel powerless. I slipped the rope in my pocket and jogged back to the lawn.

He was still sprawled where we'd left him, his head resting on the base of a Palmetto. I always thought the crèche looked so ridiculous in this little grove of palm trees imported from south Florida. Now I was about to add another eyesore to the church grounds.

I looked back to make sure Mike really had pulled the car around. The taillights glowed from around the corner. Good. Odds were he would not be cool with the whole bondage thing. It was funny; if J.B. were awake, he might have been exactly the kind of guy who could get into being tied up. As I looped the rope around his wrists—which was kind of hard to do wearing these gloves—his eyes flicked open again.

A slight smirk spread across his face.

"What are you up to, girl?" he whispered.

I leaned in, so my lips were right up against his.

"No good," I said, tightening the knot around the base of the tree. "Now be a good boy and go back to sleep."

"Okay," he nodded woozily, closing his eyes again.

I stifled a laugh. That might have been the first time J.B. ever obeyed me so blindly. I dashed another coat of lipstick on his mouth. What else did he need to complete his look? Another strand of beads? A well-placed condom? Before I knew it, I was rifling through his pockets for a pièce de résistance.

Jackpot.

My hand closed around an orange prescription bottle, which I wrestled from his jeans. Hmmm . . . J.B.'s secret fun pills strewn strategically around his passed-out body on the grass? Okay, maybe that was going too far.

I weighed the pill bottle in my hand and glanced down at his face. His eyes looked so peaceful shut. But he wasn't at peace at all; he was just so far gone that he wasn't going to remember any of this in the morning.

The weird thing was, I realized, I wanted him to remember. I wanted him to feel the embarrassment of knowing I was behind all this. He may have started the feud, but I was going to have the last laugh. I slipped the pill bottle into the pocket of Mike's tuxedo jacket.

"Maybe this will help jog your memory in the morning," I said, patting the top of his head. "Sweet dreams."

CHAPTER *Seven*

NOTHING IN HIS LIFE BECAME HIM
LIKE THE LEAVING OF IT

*A*t the edge of sleep, I am waiting in my coronation tiara and floor-length backless ecru gown. I am standing at the threshold of the Scot's Glen Golf and Country Club, waiting for the clop of horses' hooves to round the corner and take me to my Prince.

The moment comes so quickly, so easily, I can hardly remember the announcement of our win. None of this bothers me. It's going to be this moment in the carriage where everything begins.

When the horse-drawn buggy finally appears around the corner, it is even grander and glitzier than I imagined. The carriage itself is opulent, shaped like a giant silver Easter egg, and decorated with white roses and loops of twinkling lights. Even the jockey wears a white riding costume, and when he *hops down from his perch, he bows at me and opens the carriage door.*

Surprising myself, I begin to run. And in the dream, my white stiletto heels don't sink into the green of the golf course. My ladies-in-waiting don't disdain my public display of emotion. I run toward Mike, toward the celebration of our future. This carriage ride will be the one on which all future Palmetto Court carriage rides are based.

"M'lady." The jockey beams at me, kissing my white-gloved hand.

"Thank you." I smile demurely, nod my head, and let him hoist me up to my seat.

Poof.

A waft of smoke obscures my vision of the carriage's interior. And then I hear a voice:

"Change of plans, Princess."

Coughing, I wave my hands through the mist, and when the air inside the carriage clears, my jaw drops. Justin Balmer is sitting next to me where Mike is supposed to be.

Oh, it had been such a good dream until now. His black tux and emerald-green bowtie feel like they're filling up the bulk of the carriage, making me choke and making him seem bigger than life.

When he smiles at me, his green eyes bore into mine.

"Didn't I leave you at the church?" I ask, gripping the seat.

"Oh, you'll find me there again." J.B. smiles cryptically. "But I was too tied up to be much fun, and I wanted to give you some advice."

I shake my head. "News flash: We won Palmetto, and you lost. Try offering up your words of wisdom to those more pitiful than you—if you can find anyone."

"Nope," he says. "This message is for you."

His tone makes me look up at him. His mouth is set in a straight line, but his eyes are lighter, almost laughing. In a strange way, they seem to be the only thing alive about his face. They're mesmerizing and familiar at the same time.

"What are you doing?" I ask.

"Smiling," he says, "with my eyes. Remember?"

Even in the dream, my mind rolls back in time. Something about his face jars an early memory: J.B. lining up all the freshman girls before our first cotillion. He was flirtatious, trying to get everyone's eyes to "pop" seductively while our mouths were closed politely. As he moved along the row, all the other girls were giggling. I was sweating through my high-necked oxford dress. Justin stopped in front of me, and then he was the one who froze. You look familiar. Have we met?

"You still need to learn how to do it," J.B. says, holding my stare. His green eyes are potent, even as his skin goes pale and his lips turn blue.

"You can't be here," I say finally, pulling aside the white

drape curtain to look out the carriage window. I am getting claustrophobic in my carriage. "You have to go. Mike's going to show up any minute."

J.B. shakes his head, looking tired all of a sudden. And then I feel another draft of air—this time, it's freezing cold—when Justin breaks our gaze. I shiver and my skin breaks out in goose bumps.

"Like I said," he almost whispers, "there's been a change of plans."

Then he leans back in his seat and slowly closes his eyes.

"Natalie Carolina Hargrove!"

My own eyes shot open at the sound of my mom hollering up from the kitchen the next morning. I shook my head to loosen—no, to banish—the dream from my mind, but I was alarmed to find my skin still flecked with goose bumps. I pulled the covers up over my head and burrowed back into the pillow, just as my mom yelled:

"The Dukes are here. Get downstairs and eat breakfast with your future family."

Kill me now. My future *family?* That was a stretch, even for Mom. Maybe she was going to insist on going through with this unfortunate engagement, but there was no way I was ever going to consider Richard Duke or his porcine daughter Darla any kin of mine.

"Not hungry," I hollered back at my mom. If I had to be dragged to church with the Dukes and held under Palmetto-wide scrutiny, there was a limit to the additional amount of QT that I could sanely agree to spend with them. I knew breakfast with Mom's latest capital venture would mentally bankrupt me, and I needed to be on today when we pulled up to the church.

"Not good enough," my mom answered. She'd cracked open my bedroom door and poked her curler-set auburn head inside. "Can't you make the littlest effort?" she asked. "For *me?*" Mom turned down her bottom lip, an overdone pout made worse by the mauve matte lipstick she'd slathered on.

"I thought you said we were going to church," I said, taking in the rest of my mom's costume. Her highlighted bangs had been swept up, up, and up a little more in a bouffant that displayed her mastery of the tease 'n' spray, a favorite style technique among Mom's white-zin-drinking circle. Her blue eyes were lined with a silvery shadow that extended into graceful—if gaudy—cat eyes. And her red-and-white polka-dot dress hugged her curves so snugly that I could see her doing that special breathing (short quick puffs of air, à la days of corset-wearing) that she thought no one could notice. She looked great—for a Vaudeville number. But poor, sweet, trailer-transplanted Mom was still worlds away from being Palmetto pew-appropriate.

"Of course, we're going to church, honey," Mom drawled, not surprisingly oblivious. "Right after you drag your hung-over self down to a nice healthy breakfast with the Dukes."

I groaned. Since I hadn't yet moved from the bed, I wasn't sure about the degree to which my hangover was going to debilitate me—and I did not want my mother to witness that dreaded roll out of bed. After we tucked J.B. into his own rendition of a nativity scene at the church last night, Mike and I had swung by the Pitch 'n' Putt to pick up one more bottle of bubbly on the ride home. The image of J.B. waking up smothered by his boa was just too toast-worthy to go uncelebrated. But now, with Mom hovering over me, I got the feeling I was about to pay a high price for ending the night with such low-cost champagne.

I hobbled over to my mirror to survey the damage.

Ohhh, it hurt. My hair carried the distant memory of last night's ringlets, but now they were splayed in tangled chunks around my head. The glue from my fake eyelashes had left sticky blobs along my eyelids, and my lips were puffy and cracking.

"Well, you certainly smell like you had a good time last night," my mom said, holding her nose faux daintily. She sighed. "Guess your momma taught you something right."

Mom was a former Cawdor County beauty queen and a real-life beauty-school dropout. When she finally got the nerve to quit her waitressing job, Mom started working part-time at the

Charleston morgue, where she made up corpses whose families were too despondent to put up a fight. But in the past few weeks, her man-du-month had filled her head with the idea to expand her market to the living. She'd even gone as far as running business cards bearing her maiden name with the ingenious, and likely unintentionally, backhanded slogan:

Dotty Perch: You'll never look better.

Suffice it to say, Mom's little entrepreneurship had yet to really take off, but after seventeen years of being the only living recipient of her advice on how to doll-yourself-up-proper-so-you-can-get-a-man, I fully supported Mom's quest for a more receptive clientele.

Life with my kind of single mother—that is, the kind who's never actually single for long—is one unending flip-flop between parent/child and BFF. When I got my first kiss—age twelve, back corner of the bait-and-tackle shop, and yes, right next to the worms—Mom wanted to hear more dirty details than any of my friends at school.

Unfortunately, she assumed my interest in her sex life was mutual. There was a stretch of time when Mom never failed to climb into bed with me when she got dropped off the morning after a date. She'd snuggle close and fall asleep, saying she was so glad we were besties. Smoothing out the eye shadow gathered in a wet crease above her eye, I never had the heart to groan audibly enough to wake her up.

This is all to say that whenever Mom actually shifted into stern parent mode and tried, for example, to slave-drive me down to breakfast, it was hard for me to take her seriously. Sometimes I wished she could follow my philosophy about interacting with Binky. Just pick what side of the line you're on and stick with it.

Now Mom picked up a brush from my vanity and ran it through the rat's nest on top of my head. "You want a spray 'n' tease, baby? I always find that the smell of aerosol just zips the hangover right out of me."

"That's okay, Mom. I'm just going to jump in the shower."

"Okay, babylove," she kissed my forehead. "But don't forget—"

"Family breakfast, I know," I finished.

Mom gave me her relieved double blink and started for the door.

"Before you go," I said, flipping through the hangers in my closet. "I think I've got a cardigan in here that will match your dress perfectly." I pulled out the white sweater that I'd worn to dinner with the Kings and slipped it around my mother's bare shoulders. "Perfect," I said, "for church."

A half hour later, I slumped down the stairs in my variation of church attire. I was still hungover, still grouchy about being dragged to a meal with the Dukes, but at least I knew that unlike Mom, I was dressed the part of Charleston's churchgoing elite. Today I'd chosen a navy oxford shirtdress, peep-toe flats, pearls (obviously), and patterned stockings. I made a mental note to remind Mom to slip on a pair of stockings, too—even though I knew she'd resist because Richard "liked her legs unfettered."

Richard Duke. Best known in Charleston as the moneybags behind the successful florist shop, the Duke of Jessamines. Lesser known as the Dick, which Mike and I called him behind his back . . . and sometimes under our breath to his face.

I could smell the overpowering fragrance of the lilies he always brought my mother (not as chivalrous when they're *free*, Dick). I could hear the soulless box set jazz collection that he always insisted on playing.

"Dotty," he was saying to my mother, "you've outdone yourself with these cheese grits. Can I help myself to thirds?"

I could see Mom beaming when I stepped into the kitchen.

"You know, Natalie's father never liked them," she said. Her eyes met mine. "May he rest in peace."

I blanched at the phrase, thinking back to Dad's unwelcome—and still unanswered—text. Even though my mother said it every time she mentioned my poor, deceased father, this time it sounded strangely foreboding. I squinted at her. Did she know Dad was out of jail? Had he reached out to her, too?

But from the innocent look on her face as she watched the Dick spoon out the last of the grits, I knew Mom was clueless to this new development. It was almost as if Mom had convinced herself by now that her husband really did die in a sailing accident.

"There you are, Nat." The Dick stepped forward to give me a kiss. The humidity was making his comb-over act up again, and he had cheese grits in his handlebar mustache. But I knew Mom would flip if I flinched away from his lips.

"Look at you two," the Dick said, gesturing back and forth between his daughter Darla and me. "Two of Charleston's finest up-and-comings in one room." He put his arm around Mom. "How did we get so lucky?"

Darla had dressed for church in a simple yellow sheath dress whose high neckline covered her long span of cleavage. Add the frizzy dirt-brown hair and droopy earlobes she'd inherited from her father, and the Double D's dream of getting in with the inner Bambi circle at Palmetto was about as likely as Mom's desperate attempts to get the third pew status at church. Mom at least had the guts to go after what she wanted, but when it came to Darla's playing power, dull was very much an understatement.

"Did you leave Rex's early last night?" she asked me, sipping her orange juice through a straw. "I saw you cheering for J.B. at the keg stand, but I couldn't find you after that."

Who on earth would have even realized Darla was at the party last night? I glanced at Mom, who was nodding encouragingly—her eyes practically begging me to take Darla under my wing.

"I was tired," I explained. "I always like to get my beauty sleep on a church night."

"Speaking of which," Mom sang, raising a red-painted fingernail in the air, "that third pew's not getting any emptier. Everyone had enough to eat?"

I grabbed a banana for the road and threw a last-ditch pair of pantyhose at Mom, and the four of us filed out the door.

"Sorry everyone, my Porsche only fits two," the Dick said, laughing as if there was a hilarious hidden pun there. "I hope you don't mind if we take the Duke of Jessamine's van to church."

I looked at the full-size white van with the Duke of Jessamine's logo (a cartoon of Richard's face surrounded by cartoon trumpet-shaped flowers) slapped on the sliding back door. *Oh God, forgive my mother for doing this to me the week before Palmetto Court.*

I started to wonder whether maybe I deserved this little bit of karma. After all, I had stuck J.B. with that nasty walk of shame this morning. Was it just in the cosmos that I'd have to publicly descend from the Flower Van?

If my reputation at Palmetto weren't already as solid as a

tube of ChapStick in December, I might have been a little nervous. But as Dick pulled out of our driveway, I reminded myself that I was inches away from Palmetto Princess—and this little joyride was merely an example of . . . what was that old saying? Whatever doesn't kill you makes you stronger.

"Sweet Jesus," Mom gasped from the front seat when we were half a block away. "What in the Lord's name is going on at the church?"

For the first time since last night, it crossed my mind that J.B. might still be outside. I figured whoever found him first would untie him, setting him—but not his reputation—free, and that he would run shamefully home.

Now, as we turned into the lot, I prayed that last night's little prank would have worked itself out by now. Okay . . . worst case, if he was still there, I crossed my fingers that he'd at least be out of it enough not to remember how he'd gotten there.

Wait—

What were all these flashing blue lights?

What were the cops doing at church during prime dough-nut-eating time?

And why would they have called an ambulance?

My heart practically lurched into the front seat as the Dick lurched to a stop. I slung open the massive sliding door of the van to jump out of. Mom, Dick, and Darla were hot on my heels, but I didn't stop running until I reached the mass of people circled up around the Palmetto where I'd left J.B. last night. Around then, my body went completely numb.

"What happened?" I called into the buzzing crowd. "What's going on?"

Steph Merritt turned around and put a trembling hand on my shoulder. "It's J.B.," she sobbed, twitching her nose. I bit my lip, remembering that she was rumored to have been spotted in the backseat of J.B.'s Camero more than a few times this semester. I'd never had a whole lot of respect for Steph or her dark roots.

"What about J.B.?" I pressed.

"He's *dead.*"

My brain knew that my hands had flown up to my cheeks, but my body couldn't feel a thing. The world turned quiet except for a rushing sound that seemed to come from inside my head. He couldn't possibly be—

"He never went anywhere without his pills," Steph sniffed, blowing her nose on an embroidered handkerchief.

So what if J.B. had some pills on him? They were fun pills. They were party pills. They were . . . in-Mike's-jacket-pocket pills. I remembered the rush of cold air from my dream and shivered.

Mom came up behind me and stood up on her tiptoes.

"Ohhhhh, J.B., sweet boy, what happened to youuuuu?" she moaned.

I gripped her hand and squeezed it, willing her to shut up. *Don't make a scene, Mom, don't make a scene. Of course you'd be the type to fall for his charming flirty act, but now is not the time.*

But before Mom could fully overpower the rest of the crowd, the paramedics wheeled out the empty stretcher. There was something so awful about the idea of them already wheeling him away. I squeezed my eyes shut, trying not to replay the worst parts of last night in my mind. I didn't understand what was going on. Justin. Justin couldn't be dead. There was some sort of confusion, that's all.

At the sound of the whole congregation gasping at once, I opened my eyes. J.B.'s limp body popped up with the stretcher.

His skin was the color of an old bruise, dull and yellow, and his hair was matted to his forehead. He was still in the black-leather skirt and the fishnet stockings, still with that one high heel dangling from his foot.

I looked down at my hands. I had just held that ankle in them last night—and now I could hardly feel my fingers. I could hardly feel anything at all.

Just before the paramedics lifted J.B. into the ambulance, I noticed Mrs. Balmer. She hunched over her son, stroking his cheeks. She unwound the hot-pink feather boa from his dead neck and tucked it, shakily, into her purse. Then she broke down in a long, labored series of sobs until, eventually, they pulled her off his body.

I didn't realize I'd been holding my breath, and suddenly, I thought I might faint. I was looking around for some clear air and a place to sit down when I felt my phone buzz in my bag. Who could be texting at a time like this?

Doll face—don't give me the cold shoulder. Cut your dad a little slack and call me, okay? I miss you, kid.

My head spun. There was no way I could deal with my father now. Delete, I punched. Delete delete delete. I practically beat the message out of my phone. This would be my texting mantra from here on out. At least until I caught wind that Dad had ducked back out of town. At least until this awful J.B. mess had . . . settled down? What was this awful mess, anyway? I couldn't see straight. I couldn't figure it out. I was having a hard time grasping for breath.

Behind me, I heard someone say, "Thus endeth the competition for Palmetto's throne."

Rex Freeman's loud voice was cheerless when he chimed in, "Looks like you've pretty much got Prince locked down now, huh, King?"

Mike. Where was he? I needed him. He needed me. I swayed. My eyes raced through the crowd to find my love my love my love—

There. Mike was standing stoically across the circle in his church suit. He was flanked by his parents, stroking Diana's hand.

But he was looking straight at me.

I started toward him in a hot rush through the crowd, feeling alive again, feeling the blood pour back through my body. My heart was hammering so hard I thought my ribs might break. I needed to get to him. Mike would know what to do.

He shook his head and narrowed his dark eyes as I approached. A chill ran down my spine as he mouthed, "Nat, what did you do?"

CHAPTER *Eight*

AN ABSOLUTE TRUST

On Monday morning, I went through an entire pack of Juicy Fruit gum during the twenty-minute drive to school. With an aching jaw and a sinking feeling in my stomach, I parked in my usual spot under the leaning Palmetto. I got out of the car and had to follow suit by leaning on the driver's door for support. Sweat poured down the back of my neck. How was I going to make it inside?

Suddenly, I got a little extra push from Ms. Cafiero, my mustache-sprouting eight-period algebra teacher who practically hauled me toward the front steps by the earlobe.

"Wait, I never meant—" I started to confess.

"Save it," she interrupted, grabbing the kid in the car next door by the earlobe too and shoving us both in the direction of the auditorium.

"Do not pass go," Ms. Caf commanded. "Do not collect two hundred dollars. Go to the assembly. Go directly to the assembly."

"But I have shop class," the kid beside me whined.

"Not today, you don't," Caf snapped. "A fellow student loses his life in a freak accident. I think your model airplane can wait."

A freak accident. That's what the school was calling it. It was the first piece of non-terrifying news I'd heard since yesterday morning when my whole world fell apart. I needed to know more before I went inside. If I could just make a pit stop at the junior bathroom to pay Tracy Lampert a visit. . . .

"Nature calls," I tried on Ms. Cafiero, failing to edge my way around her Botticelli hips.

"Well, you're going to have to hold it," Ms. Cafiero frowned, steering my tense shoulders into the assembly hall. I held my breath and stumbled inside.

Once I crossed the threshold into the large, high-ceilinged auditorium, I was hit with a rush of semi-comforting déjà vu. I'd practically come of age in this room. It was one of those chameleon venues, a catch-all for Palmetto's big-ticket events. We held the final pep rally here before the homecoming game each fall. We'd squirmed in these seats last year listening to the creepy male gynecologist they'd flown in from the CDC when a rash of STDs swept the school. We'd even sold out the place the night Mike played Marcus Antonius in last spring's performance of *Julius Caesar*. But never had I heard such a buzz in the auditorium as the one I walked into this morning.

Everyone was wearing black. A few of the junior girls even had dark veils covering their faces. I looked down, suddenly grateful that my dark gray cowl-neck cashmere would pass for the mourning attire that was suddenly what people wore at Palmetto.

And it wasn't just the costumes that were wigging me out. The whole energy of the room seemed to swarm as kids darted in and out of conversations, up and down the aisles. No one could sit still. We looked like a colony of ants who'd just had our farm kicked over.

Chaos made me dizzy. I reached into my purse for more gum and remembered I was already out. My jaw throbbed. I wanted Tracy and I wanted Mike. Was I really going to have to wade through this sea of sobbing Bambies to find them?

Up ahead, I spotted Kate's long hair glimmering under the florescent gym lights. I sidled toward her, and the sophomore foursome huddled around her. They were all sharing a box of tissues, like it was popcorn.

"What if he's gone for good?" Kate moaned to the other girls. I had to do a double take to realize she was *crying*.

"You have to prepare for the worst," Steph Merritt jumped in, helping Kate to blow her nose.

Jesus. How much more proof did these kids need? Kate hardly even knew J.B. I know it sounded weird for me to feel protective over his death, but I had known him. I *had* known him a little too well. Hadn't I earned the right?

"What, he didn't look dead enough yesterday morning?" I blurted too harshly, too quickly. The other girls almost jumped back in surprise, but Kate just sniffed without judgment.

"We're not talking about J.B.," she said. "Haven't you heard about Baxter?"

"What about him?" I said quickly, glancing around the auditorium.

Kate gave the girls an apologetic frown and stepped forward to take me by the arm. She led me a few feet away toward relative quiet.

"Baxter's phone," Kate shuddered. "It's been shut off all weekend. I'm so lame; I must have tried him twenty times yesterday." She looked at me. "He said we were going to study."

"So he didn't call you back," I shrugged. "That could mean anything. Maybe he hired a tutor—"

"But Saturday night . . ." She blushed and looked away. "We kind of . . . at the party . . ."

I sighed and rubbed my temples. I could feel the tension mounting in my skull.

"Kate, do you have any idea how many senior guys at this school sleep with sophomores only to blow them off?" I asked.

Kate opened her mouth to speak and shook her head. Tears sprung to her eyes. I hadn't meant to make her cry, but usually her skin was thicker than it was today.

"I'm sorry," I said, squeezing her shoulder. "I didn't mean it like that. I'm just freaked out about the J.B. news. I shouldn't have—"

"It's okay," she said quietly. "I'm freaked out, too. One of the partners at my father's firm heard Justin was D.O.A. by sunrise on Sunday morning. He was already gone when the grounds-keeper called the paramedics. Baxter, I mean. They're pinning J.B.'s death on a bad combination of drugs. But—" She glanced up and her lip quivered. She gave me the most tortured look.

"But what?" I asked, feeling yesterday's numb tingle wash over me again.

Kate leaned in to whisper. "But Baxter's not at school today," she said. "And now the juniors are saying he might have had something to do with what happened."

"I'm sure it's purely speculation," I said, knowing full well that Tracy Lampert never speculated.

Kate shook her head. "No, they're talking about this video Baxter was filming that night. The juniors said J.B.'s in a lot of the footage on the DVD, and if the cops get a hold of it . . ."

She trailed off, but my overactive imagination kicked right in. Kate had been there when Baxter was egging J.B. on from the library balcony during the keg stands. If he had a DVD full of J.B. footage, who could blame those brilliant juniors for putting the pieces together?

"Where's the DVD now?" I asked.

Kate shook her head and blew her nose. She didn't know anything else.

It was time for a more reliable source of information. I stood up on a chair to get a better aerial view of the room. With so many small groups of students-turned-mourners clustered together, the auditorium looked like a convening of witches.

Finally, in the back corner, I spotted Tracy and her minions. They were huddling up around someone so closely that I couldn't quite make out . . . Mike. Well, two birds, one stone. I hopped down from the chair and started to beeline toward them. But then I heard the infamous triple gavel rap of Principal Glass. He was calling us to order.

I know delusions of grandeur are not unusual in high school, but usually they're limited to quarterbacks with God complexes—not the faculty. But after our last principal was hauled away on house arrest, Palmetto was blessed with the kind of temporary fill-in whose big dreams of sitting on the Supreme Court were smashed after, oh, the fifth time he failed the South Carolina bar exam.

It was obvious, as Principal Glass stood behind the podium in his tweed and his toupee, that lording over a bunch of high school kids with a gavel was his small way of coming to terms with his life's shortcomings.

"All sit," he boomed into the microphone, rapping the gavel until everyone lowered the pitch of their gossip to at least a whisper. I was still a good five rows away from Mike and Tracy. Too far. I *had* to get there before the assembly started.

"I suggest you find a seat."

Ms. Cafiero had appeared out of nowhere to thwart me again. I was losing patience for this lady fast, but when I considered the likelihood of making it past her with both my earlobes intact, I gave up and sank into the nearest seat.

To my left was June Rattler (of the unforgettable tuba-blowing Palmetto Court poster), and to my right was Ari Ang (the Anger of the mysterious green beaker). Ugh. I could not have special-ordered a lowlier crew for gossip potential.

"A great tragedy took place this weekend, as some of you may know," Principal Glass began, waving the gavel with that this-is-gonna-be-a-long-one air.

Thirteen minutes into the world's most transparent speech about the sanctity of life, I was at the end of my already frazzled wits. Everyone knew that the administration at Palmetto (called the "fishbowl" for the glass walls around their cluster of offices) had only ever seen J.B. as a thorn in their collective thigh.

If Principal Glass had known anything about the school he was "running," he would know that Palmetto was a place that

fed, cleansed, and healed itself on the therapeutic powers of
the rumor mill. If we were going to get past J.B.'s accident, it
was going to happen in whispered corners in the hallways, not
under the bang of Glass's gavel.

"In conclusion," he droned, "I must stress the importance
of carrying on with our daily lives." By now, he had to raise
his voice over the rustling of students taking their cue to grab
their bags.

"Which is why I remind you that the Nutritional Fair will
still take place at lunch today." Louder still, he shouted, rapping his gavel as the room began to clear out, "And don't forget
to cast your votes for the Palmetto Prince and Princess today.
We will mourn the loss of Justin Balmer, but we will carry on
as a school."

That last tidbit of advice fell on an almost empty auditorium. It was probably for the best—even though Palmetto
Court and J.B.'s death were scarily intertwined in my brain, I
didn't exactly want the rest of the school to relate.

Back in the crowded hallway, I raced to find Mike.

"Thank God," I said, wrapping myself in his arms. "What'd
you hear from Tracy?" I blurted.

Whoa. That was not the first thing I meant to say.

"I mean—how are you?"

Mike looked at me strangely.

"Didn't you get my texts?" he asked. "We need to talk."

Crap. I closed my eyes. Ever since that second text from my dad yesterday, I'd been deleting all my text messages, sight unseen.

"I'm sorry," I said, pressing my face into his chest. "My phone's been . . . acting up. I didn't—"

I stopped stammering when Mike put his hand on my shoulder.

"Nat," he said. It was then that I noticed he was trembling.

But Mike could bench-press more than anyone at school. He broke three state football records as a JV player. Not once, in all our years of watching horror movies, had I ever seen him flinch. If my life depended on it, I would have sworn that Mike King didn't know *how* to tremble. But now, his navy sweater quaked, and I left my head there, as if there were a way for me to absorb his panic. I lifted my head up and tried to smile up at his brown eyes. Then I took his broad, strong hands in mine and held them to my heart.

"Baby," I said, "look at me. Hold me. Listen to me. We don't even know if what happened was our fault."

Mike swallowed hard and shook his head. I held his chin in place between two fingers and whispered, "We have to hold it together, at least until we know more. I know there's a lot on our plates right now. Once we win Palmetto, we have to focus on the coronation speech. There's the student body to thank and—"

"Coronation? Are you kidding? That speech is the least of our worries," Mike said through clenched teeth. "Nat, I'm freaking out."

"The coronation speech is *not* the least of our worries," I huffed, as quietly as I could. "Don't you see? It's more important now than ever that we keep up the pretense that everything is okay."

Mike glanced around the hallway. "We shouldn't talk like this out here."

I watched him eye the janitor's closet behind us and saw the quick nod he did when he was making an impulse decision. He opened the door and pulled me inside.

But . . . we always went outside under the bleachers or to our secret waterfall above the Cove to talk. We didn't duck into dank janitorial closets with blinking red EXIT lights and empty garbage cans. Everything about this moment was wrong.

"What happened when I was in the car?" Mike asked, closing the door.

"Nothing—"

"*Nat*," he interrupted.

"I may have loosely tied him to the tree."

Mike pressed his forehead to the wall, away from me.

"Did you give him anything? Any drugs?"

"Of course not," I said. "What do you think I am?" I was

starting to get defensive. "In fact, I took some pills *off* his hands. He should probably thank me that when the cops found him, he was clean."

Mike whipped around.

"What did you take?"

"I don't know," I shrugged. "Whatever was in his pocket. I just stuck it in your jacket. I was cold. I forgot about it. I mean, I have your jacket right he—"

Before I could even unzip my backpack all the way, Mike had grabbed his jacket from it and was rummaging through the pockets. When he yanked out the little orange bottle, he looked at me wide-eyed.

"What?" I asked—as if playing dumb might undo my mistake.

Mike crouched under the blinking red light to examine the label.

"Trileptal," he read slowly. "Indications: nerve-damage relief and seizure prevention. Take one pill every six hours." He squinted to read the fine print. "Seek medical attention upon missed dosage."

"I thought they were fun pills," I stammered. "I thought he'd never miss them."

Mike glared at me as he stuffed the suit jacket into his backpack. Then he thrust the pill bottle into my sweaty, shaky palm.

In a voice lower than I'd ever heard him use, he said, "Lose these."

CHAPTER *Nine*

THE FRUITLESS CROWN

"Nat, I swear, if you don't stay still, I'll never get this eyelash on, and then you'll be all lopsided."

How did I get here?

I was seated on a wicker pedestal facing the bulb-lit bridal vanity. The peach-toned ladies locker room of the Scot's Glen Golf and Country Club was full of my ladies-in-waiting from school. Amy Jane hovered to my right, waiting to glue the last in a box of twenty individual fake eyelashes to the outer corners of my eye. Jenny stood over me, her seven-gauge ceramic curling iron poised in the air. Behind us, the gaggle of underclassmen handmaids slung over giant floor pillows, buffing their nails and begging me with their liquid-lined eyes to be given a job to do.

This was what I'd been waiting for. But . . .

It was Wednesday afternoon, just before the coronation ceremony for Palmetto Prince and Princess. By Tuesday morning, even before the vote, the whole school had known it was going to be a landslide, but since they'd left J.B.'s name on the ballot in memoriam, they waited until after the official day of mourning to announce our win. Even then, it wasn't official until Principal Glass called us into his office yesterday to break the news with his killjoy bravado.

"Now just a quick acceptance speech from each of you tomorrow," he said, his eyes looking past us like he was following a script. "Remember, the Ball is still ten days away, so kindly hold the party reins in until then. Tomorrow's just a small, *family-friendly* affair."

He cracked open a can of Coke and split it between three Styrofoam cups as if to drive home his crusade against substance abuse.

"To the Prince and Princess," he said.

"Cheers," I said, raising my cup and keeping my eyes on Principal Glass so I wouldn't be able to tell if Mike's hand shook.

"There," Amy Jane now said, stepping back to view her masterpiece. She held a mirror up for me to see. "You're fairer than a flower."

"And deadlier than a snake."

I spun around. The mirror tumbled out of my hand and shattered on the floor.

"Who said that?" I hissed.

For a moment, no one spoke. Then Darla Duke penitently got to her knees and clasped her hands.

"I didn't I just," she stammered. "It's just something my grandmother used to say: 'Look like a flower, act like a snake,' or something. It's supposed to be a good thing."

The words tumbled from her mouth. Lies. Lies. Lies. Useless shrugs and lies.

"It means you know how to get what you want," she kept blathering.

"Well, I don't have to tell you what my grandmother told me about broken mirrors," Jenny butted in crisply. "Someone clean this up."

I looked at Darla, keeping my voice low so it would stay even. "Yes, we don't want anyone getting hurt."

While Darla and three other Bambies jumped up to scoop up the shards of glass, Kate stood up and leaned in to me. We hadn't spoken since Monday when she clued me in about *Baxter*.

"You okay?" she asked. "You seem a little—"

"Just nervous," I said. "About the acceptance speech."

"Of course," she nodded—even though Kate had seen me destroy last year's finalists in Palmetto debate tournaments.

Public speaking was one of my strongest suits. It had to be: As Palmetto Princess, I'd be the official voice behind the mic at every pep rally and award ceremony for the next year.

As I watched Kate empathetically brush my hair in the mirror, I realized she would know I wasn't nervous about the speech. She knew that I'd perfected my coronation speech as far back as this time last year, when Marc Wise and Sadie Hoagland took the crown. It was all memorized, from the pride-of-Charleston theme behind our campaign, right down to whom to thank and in what order. It wasn't the speech that was wigging me out—it was the nightmare I'd had about this carriage ride.

"Oh," Kate said, interrupting my thoughts. "Your mom swung by and brought this over." She unsheathed a bright orange-matte tube of lipstick that my mom had been trying to get me to wear since she first put full makeup on me for the fourth-grade piano recital. It was the kind of color Mom could usually only get her corpses to agree to wear. I shuddered.

"That's what I thought," Kate said, whipping out a much less terrifying shade of shimmery pink. She showed me the name on the bottom of the tube. "See that?" she pointed. It was called Princess.

But when she dotted the lipstick around my mouth and held out the tissue for me to blot, all I could think about was the lipstick I'd put on J.B.

I went utterly cold.

The lipstick. The bound wrists. The pill bottle.

"The carriage!" the Bambies exclaimed from the corner. All of them dashed to the window. "The carriage is here! It's outside!"

"Tell me you went with the vanilla-flavored massage oil I suggested," Amy Jane said, coming up behind me to add a few more sprays of Aqua Net to my updo.

But there was no massage oil in the montage I was trying to stop from running through my mind. There were just J.B.'s blue lips in the carriage and the icy chill I'd felt when he'd closed his eyes in my dream.

There's been a change of plans, he'd said.

I needed to get out to the real carriage to prove to myself it had only been a nightmare—or at least that *part* of it had only been a nightmare. I needed to get on top of Mike and take a break from my J.B. paranoia. But when I stood up, just when I needed to show strength, I teetered in my sling-back heels, then collapsed on the vanity chair.

"Jesus, Nat, you're white as a ghost. More rouge!" Amy Jane called over for reinforcements. "What is it, honey? Talk to us."

"I forgot to lose it," I mumbled, thinking about the pills still tucked inside the inner pocket of my backpack. "Mike told me to lose it and I didn't."

"What's she talking about?" Jenny whispered to Amy Jane. "I don't get it."

"Oh my God," Amy Jane said. "Were you and Mike going to play 'revirginized' in the carriage? You guys *are* kinky."

Before I could say anything to cover up my slip about the pills, my two ladies-in-waiting had helped me to my feet. Minutes later, they were guiding me out the door towards the carriage. I noticed Kate hung back.

"Listen, don't freak out," Jenny said, looking me in the eye. "You and Mike are the real deal. You don't need to break any school records out there. Just be yourself," she said.

Amy Jane slipped something into my hand. It was the same size and shape as the pill bottle, but when I looked down—

"I knew you'd forget the massage oil," she laughed. "I always carry extra."

I started walking slowly toward the carriage. It wasn't nearly as glitzy as the carriage in my dream, which was nothing less than an enormous relief. It was the same old wooden painted carriage that they'd been using for as long as there'd been Palmetto Princesses. The driver looked normal enough, too, faded jeans and a black blazer. But when he opened the door and held out a hand to help me up, his forehead was creased with worry lines.

"I'm sorry, miss, but I was told to let you know." He fidgeted with the buttons on his blazer. "He isn't coming."

What? I stuck my head inside the plush red-velvet carriage. It was empty.

I looked back at the girls' faces, huddled giddily in the window. I had no choice. I waved back like nothing was wrong.

"Just drive," I said to the coachman through gritted teeth.

It was a too-sunny day on the golf course, and I couldn't figure out how to get the blinds down inside the carriage. By the time we rounded the fourteenth hole, I'd bitten off all my fingernails and steam was coming out of my ears. In a dumb move that showed how out of it I was, I'd left my Juicy Fruit in my bag. I had nothing to help calm me down after being stood up by Mike. How could he? In front of the entire school and everyone's families? I was going to absolutely kill—

Someone was knocking on the carriage door. I shoved myself up against the window . . . and saw him. Mike was running alongside the carriage to keep up.

"Stop the coach!" I cried.

Before the horses had even slowed to a cantor, Mike swung open the door and climbed in. "I'm so sorry," he said, leaning over to kiss me.

I was still too furious and too stunned to move.

"I tried to call. I knew you'd be freaking out. I just . . . I needed some time to think about how to go through with this after . . ." He took my hands.

I waved a hand to cut him off. "Groveling later, mental

preparation now. We have exactly three minutes to get in the royal mindset." I handed Mike a printout of the coronation speech. "Your paragraphs are in blue; mine are in pink, okay?"

"Um," Mike said. "Actually—"

"We're here!" I cried, looking out the window at the vine-coated trellis marking our entrance. Before we knew it, the coachman opened the door. He let out a low whistle as he helped me to the ground.

"I've been driving this rig to the coronation for a lot of years," he said quietly. "The stunt your guy pulled today, Princess, was a first. Don't let him off the hook too easy, okay?"

I looked at Mike. "Oh, I won't."

On the lawn, a yawning string quartet began to play but was soon overshadowed by the cheers of the crowd, calling out our names and waving loyally. Mike said nothing, just reached for my hand. We walked down the golden carpet to the stage.

The funny thing was, everything looked just like I had imagined, just like I'd planned out in my head all these years. There was my mother, in her tight Jessamine-print tube dress and high heels, tears in her eyes, hand in the Dick's. There were the Kings on the other side of the stage, smiling closed-mouth smiles and wearing expensive silk suits in corresponding muted shades. There were the last few years of Palmetto

Court alumni flanking either side of the stage, including Phillip Jr. and Isabelle. There were all our friends, dressed to impress, eyes wide in expectation of hearing our speeches— and our carriage ride sexploits at the reception.

The only part of the vision that wasn't just as I imagined was us: the Prince and Princess of Palmetto. We were hand in hand, but I felt like Mike and I were worlds apart.

At the podium, he leaned in to kiss my cheek. His lips felt dry and rough. I closed my eyes and tried to enjoy the crowd's polite applause.

"Thank you all," Mike said when they'd died down. He cleared his throat and looked down at the speech I'd printed out for him. Then he slid it into his inner jacket pocket and pulled out a napkin scribbled with notes. I reached forward to stop him, but he gripped my hand so tightly, I would have made a scene if I moved.

"You've all heard these acceptance speeches many times before," Mike began. "Some of you," he gestured behind us at the Courts of Palmetto's past, "have even given them yourselves. So you know the drill, and you also know how grateful and excited Natalie and I are to accept this honor." He scanned the crowd and squeezed my hand even tighter. "But today is about something else, and we would be wrong not to acknowledge the passing of a good friend and a great man."

Don't do this, Mike, don't do this.

"The man who should have been Prince," he said.

No he didn't.

"So in lieu of our acceptance speeches—"

No he wouldn't!

"Natalie and I would like to ask for a moment of silent prayer, and then we'll move right to the reception. We'll see you all tomorrow at the funeral."

I opened my mouth to respond, but when I looked at Mike, I knew: Everything we'd spent so long preparing for Palmetto Court was gone.

CHAPTER *Ten*

BLACK AND DEEP DESIRES

"*A*shes to ashes, dust to dust."

On Thursday afternoon, still nursing the wound of my usurped speech at the coronation, I stood shoulder to Mike's broad shoulder in the graveyard behind the church. We watched the pallbearers lower J.B.'s body into the ground.

"Whenever we are faced with such a tragic and unlucky loss," the rarely somber Minister Clover droned from his staticky, clip-on microphone, "the community is, quite literally, seized with grief."

My head shot up at the choice of the word *seize*. The whole funeral had felt so dull and generic up until that point. Clover was notorious for his bad puns during sermons. Was he actually making a reference to J.B.'s medical condition?

Then I wondered: Did anyone besides Justin's immediate

family—and now me and Mike—even know about his medical condition? I looked around at the downward-gazing, hands-clasped congregants but saw no glimmer of recognition in their faces. I thought back to Steph Merritt, honking her nose in the handkerchief and mentioning something about his pills—but it was obvious that she hadn't really known the truth. I didn't get what it was about death that made all these people wail at the funeral of someone they'd never *really* known.

My eyes fell on J.B.'s older brother Tommy, whose arms encased his weeping mother. For a second, I thought it looked like he was glaring at the minister's word choice, but then it started to rain again, and a sea of black umbrellas popped up around the funeral. The musty smell of wet vinyl wafted over everything, and it was hard to see much more besides the giant white steeple rising up like a landmark in front of us.

In the bathroom before the funeral, I'd been smoothing out my ponytail when I came across three Bambies huddled together, crying. These were girls who only yesterday had been trembling with vicarious titillation as they watched me get escorted into the horse-drawn carriage.

I'd always known girls from the South could get a bad rap for being kind of saccharine, but Palmetto should have taken out a patent on its own brand of artificiality. These girls could change their attitudes more quickly than their clothes and never look worse for the wear. Everything depended on the venue and on whom they needed to impress.

I'd rolled my eyes at them in the bathroom, but it was mostly because even though I wanted to, somehow I couldn't bring myself to cry about J.B. In fact, I couldn't bring myself to do much these days. I couldn't answer that nagging text from my dad, still lurking in my mental inbox. I couldn't even relish my coronation—though I did have Mike to blame for that. But most disturbingly, for some reason, I still couldn't bring myself to get rid of that bottle of pills.

I wasn't going to *swallow* them. They were just an important reminder that I'd gotten us into this, and I would get us out.

But as I watched the black-suited men dump the black earth over the black coffin, piling it higher and higher to cover the big black hole, I started to feel claustrophobic, almost like I was inside that coffin with J.B. My umbrella hovered like a cage over my head. The itchy neckline of my dress constricted my throat so much that I could barely swallow. I leaned my head out from under the umbrella, but the drizzle and fog were hanging so low to the ground that it felt like even the sky was caving in on me. My chest heaved as I choked on the rain. I couldn't breathe.

Mike put his arm around my shoulder—more suffocation—and started to guide me back inside the church. It was over. I saw my mom waving from the doorway. I couldn't bear to listen to her ask me whether I thought J.B.'s coloring had looked natural at the open casket.

"I can't breathe," I said to Mike. "I need air."

He took my hand. "Okay, let's take a walk."

"I'm still mad at you," I said.

He didn't answer. We tramped through the soggy cemetery, past the Cyprus trees with their billowing gray trunks, and away from the melodrama of the crowd. Soon there was just the white noise of the rain. I knew where Mike was leading us. His feet just went there naturally.

We stopped in front of his family's lineup of plots in the center of the graveyard. I followed Mike inside the walk-in mausoleum where Grandfather and Grandmother King were buried. I had been there one time before, two summers ago on the fifth anniversary of his grandfather's death. The mausoleum had seemed creepy enough to me then, full of living people in the middle of a hot, sunny day.

Now the two of us ducked like zombies under the low cement doorway. We took a seat on the carved marble bench. The dank smell of Spanish moss filled my nose and made me cough. I might have been scared if I had stopped listening to the thunder and keeping my eyes on the large stamped KING printed over entrance of the mausoleum. Mike ran his hand in circles over my back. It was hard to stay mad at him in here.

We hadn't said a word since we left the funeral. In fact,

we hadn't said much to each other since Mike's big speech yesterday, except for a few polite remarks made for public consumption at the reception. Come to think of it, we hadn't really talked since . . . well, since before J.B.

I had friends who stressed about lulling into a pause in conversation with a guy on the phone or during a dinner date at MacB's. I'd always felt bad for them for missing the point. Mike and I didn't have awkward silences; we had intimate ones. Kate would look at me like I was insane whenever I'd talk about how much I loved to be quiet next to him. But maybe this hush was stretching it, even for us.

I opened my mouth, sure that I'd have something of interest to say, but when I hung there gaping for too long, Mike said, "I wish this rain could wash everything we did away."

"It can't."

Both of us sounded like robots.

"Justin's dead," I continued, feeling the impact of those two awful words fill up the mausoleum. "We can't ever undo that."

My mind was whirling with thoughts of J.B.'s smug face, the bragging manner he took on whenever he smiled. I wanted to stop thinking about him, stop getting those flashes of his green eyes. It made me wonder what exactly Mike was thinking just then but not saying.

On my left, he sighed. "Maybe we have to come clean."

"What?" I gasped, whipping my head around.

Mike rubbed his eyes like a kid someone forgot to put to bed. His shoulders seemed to cave in around his chest.

"This thing is driving me insane. I haven't slept in four days. They're going to find out what we did."

"No, they're not," I said, turning my head away so I wouldn't have to stare at how small he seemed right then.

"I left my water bottle in his *hands*—"

I shook my head. "Mike, every guy your year has that exact same Nalgene. And all the Bambies think it's cool to buy them, too. We can skirt that evidence easily."

"But someone will have seen us leave the party with Balmer practically halfdead already. What's it going to look like if we try to cover it up until they find us? Let's just come clean. We'll say we didn't mean for things to get so—"

"No." I stood up and started pacing. There was a square cutout in the cement that looked back at the church, and I could see the funeral-goers heading out toward the parking lot. They'd all go back to their quiet little homes and spark the phone lines with their gossip. But if we came clean, what would I go back to?

My old trailer-park world with no way out? The muck of my past life? I could almost smell the rotting-fish stench right now. Girls like me didn't get a second chance. This was it. My lips quivered, and I could feel my shoulders start to shake.

Mike sighed and reached his hand out for me. "Look, I don't want to go to jail any more than you do."

Who said anything about jail? I suddenly realized that Mike had no idea what I was thinking. I filled his open hand with mine.

"Then we fix this, Mike. We just do."

He looked up at me. "How?"

"Starting at the source of all Palmetto intel," I said, forcing my mind to keep up with my tongue. "The rumor mill. What have we heard so far?"

Mike shrugged and exhaled. He was never one to get too caught up in the mill. "Something about that footage Baxter Quinn shot at the party."

I smacked my palm against my forehead. "You're a genius," I said, surprised to find myself laugh in spite of our dire straits. "They've already picked out the man for us. He's still missing, by the way."

"Wait . . . do you mean . . ." Mike shook his head, incredulous. "We blame Baxter?"

"Why not?" I said, trying to sound nonchalant, even though I could feel my voice breaking. "Just plant a few clues."

"Hold on." Mike dropped my hand and rubbed his forehead, the way he did when he was cramming for a big test. "First we accidentally . . . kill someone. Now you want to frame someone *else?*"

"No, no, no," I cooed, standing up and stepping in between his legs. I rubbed my fingers in a slow circle around his temples. "It wouldn't exactly be framing. You saw Baxter that night. He was handing out drugs left and right. We both heard him say someone should cut J.B. off—then twenty minutes later, he's cheering on the second keg stand from the balcony."

"I don't know," Mike grimaced. "Baxter's no saint, but he's not a murderer."

"We don't have to make him a murderer. We just have to clear our names by shifting the focus somewhere else. Look," I said, lowering my forehead so that it was touching his, "we can't bring J.B. back."

There it was again. The icy feeling I now got whenever I really thought about J.B.'s death. This time, it was so strong I almost cried out in pain. But then I looked at Mike's furrowed brow—which meant the window for persuasion was closing. I wrapped my arms around my chest to fight the chill and made myself keep going.

"All we can do is uphold our reputations as ambassadors of goodwill during our school's time of need," I said finally.

"I guess you're right," Mike nodded.

"Of course, I'm right."

"It's not like Baxter ever even comes to class. If *he* got expelled . . ." he trailed off.

"Exactly," I said. "Isn't it better to hold our heads high and let the police punish someone who deserves to be hauled away, anyway? We can't go down for this, Mike." I covered my heart with my hands. "Now more than ever, Palmetto needs its Prince and Princess."

"Well," Mike said, giving me a small smile and pulling me onto his lap, "I know I need my Princess."

It felt like centuries since we'd been this close. I couldn't help it; I gave in to his lips and, for the first time all week, I relaxed.

"Something's poking me and it's not, um, me," Mike said, adjusting himself over me on the marble slab. He pointed toward my hip. When I realized where he was going, I grabbed his hand.

"Don't," I said.

He wrestled free and went for the side pocket of my raincoat.

"What do you have in there?" he asked quickly.

When he pulled out J.B.'s pill bottle, his face screwed up like he'd eaten something bad. "What are you still doing with these?"

"I don't know," I stammered. Why couldn't I just tell Mike the truth? Oh yeah, because it sounded *crazy*.

"Me neither," he said, incredulous. "I thought we agreed you would lose them." He stood up and ran his fingers through his hair. "You act like you have this all figured out, and then you can't hide the most obvious piece of evidence? What if someone catches you with this?"

"It's not like I can just throw it out at home," I said. Mike was well aware that ever since Mom started screwing the Dick and got all into composting his gardens, she had the maid pick through our trash like a hobo. I reached for the pills in his hand. "I'm just waiting for the right place to get rid of them. I'll take care of it, I promise."

"If we screw this up—"

I leaned forward to put a hand over his mouth.

"Do you love me?" I asked.

"Come on," he sighed, sitting back down.

"Do you love me?" I said again, holding my breath.

Mike looked up with his is-the-South-swampy smile and said, "I just tackled you in my grandfather's mausoleum when we have a homicide to cover up," he said, kissing the top of my head. "I might be, literally, crazy about you."

Relief washed over me. "Then we can't screw up," I said. "We just have to stay strong, together." I sat back down on his lap, putting my arms around his neck. "I'll talk to Tracy Monday morning. And—I'll get rid of the pills. You get the scoop on Baxter's DVD from the guys."

Before Mike had a chance to look nervous again, I straddled him, hiking up my black dress around my waist.

I wrapped my legs around his torso, taking care that the pill bottle didn't come between us again, and I leaned in to whisper in his ear.

"You have to want this as much as you want me."

Mike sighed into my hair. The warmth of his breath on my neck felt so comforting.

"Okay, Nat," he moaned softly. "We'll nail Baxter."

CHAPTER *Eleven*

AT ODDS WITH MORNING

On Sunday morning, I lay in my canopy bed surrounded by the remnants of one of Mom's white frilly pillow projects—and the ghosts of my testosterone-filled past. I had J.B.'s seizure meds in one hand and my cell phone opened to my dad's third unanswered text in the other hand. Two men I thought I'd rid myself of, two signs that I'd been very wrong indeed. I looked back and forth from one hand to the other, feeling utterly trapped between them.

If I was as strong as I dared Mike to be, I could not give these men a free pass to unhinge me. No. I had to unhinge them.

Reminding myself that I was merely revising—not actually breaking—the vow of silence I took against my dad back when he skipped town, I hit the compose button on my phone.

I needed to send the kind of message I wouldn't have had the courage to send back then, when the vow of silence was as far as I could go.

Save the 'Daddy's home' charade and just spit out what you want.

I tried to imagine his reaction, the way the wrinkles around his silverfish eyes would fall slack—but the point was not to think of him. The point was to think of myself.

Send.

It took a moment to realize that my heart wasn't racing. I was calm and collected. Okay. One talisman down, one to go.

My father had been haunting me because I let him. Now, with J.B.'s coffin still fresh in the ground, I only hoped I could put him to rest as well.

I'd spent the past week fumbling with the prescription bottle, and I guess my palms had been sweatier than usual because the label was starting to peel off. I tugged at the sticker, and before I knew it, the whole label came off in my hand.

Oh crap. Had I just multiplied the evidence? Or—had I made it easier to dispose of? Mom had a paper shredder downstairs (a divorcee's best friend, she liked to say)—but I couldn't risk a run-in with her. Better to be my own paper shredder.

I dashed to the bathroom and hunched over the salmon-colored toilet bowl, snipping the label into flushable-size pieces. They fell into the bowl like feathers, and soon I couldn't make out the word anti-seizure at all.

All week, I'd been wondering whether someone at Palmetto would leak the details about J.B.'s condition, but the actual cause of his death seemed to still be a public mystery. I guess it didn't surprise me. As interested as they were in the classic southern facade of perfection, J.B.'s family would be exactly the type to want to keep his seizures on the down low. Maybe when I flushed the toilet, I would just be following their lead.

Now about the actual pills. All I had to do was flush them, too. As soon as the tank filled up, I'd just hold them upside down over the bowl and free myself of them.

My wrist hovered over the toilet. I was trembling . . . okay, now full-on quaking.

I couldn't do it.

I sunk down over the bowl and laid my head in my hands. I'd tried to seem so unruffled yesterday in front of Mike, but alone, I guess I still couldn't accept what I'd done. These pills were all I had left of J.B., and maybe I needed to let them go in a more ceremonial way. In some sort of tribute instead of in a toilet. Like the therapist Mom made me see when Dad left used to say: It was all about finding your own kind of closure. What form exactly that kind of closure would take, I still had no idea.

"Natalie."

Shit. My mom's head was poking through my bedroom door. In seconds, she'd be close enough to see what I was holding. I stuffed my hands and the bottle in the pocket of my Palmetto sweatshirt and turned around.

"The Dukes are here. Get your coat; we're leaving," she said, straightening her cropped bright-pink top over her pink-and-yellow-checkered pedal pushers.

I groaned to remember. This week's "family fun day" with the Dukes was going to be a whopper. The other day, the Dick declared that he was in the market for some new real estate in the Cove—the way other people declare they're in the market for a new spring hat—and now we all had to go house hunting.

For Mom, today was about playing her cards right in hopes of squeezing something sizable out of him—which, from what I gathered about the Dick, probably didn't happen often in the bedroom. For me, today meant suffering in silence.

But before Mom could steer me out of my room, there was a timid knock on the door. Darla stuck her mouse head through the frame.

"Um, Nat," she said, looking nervous, "would it be okay if I . . . I spilled some yogurt on my shirt." She held her pale-blue baby tee out from her torso to prove that the yogurt spill was indeed true. "My dad thought, maybe . . ."

"Of course, Natalie has something you can borrow," Mom

butted in, putting her hand on Darla's shoulder, as if this were a happy bonding moment for everyone. "Right, Nat?"

Darla's mouth was set in a perpetual gape, making her look like one of the fish piled up on the Cawdor wharf. Not exactly the type I wanted modeling my wardrobe as we drove all around the Coveted in broad daylight. Something scrubbier would be more her style, anyway.

"Here," I said, starting to pull my Palmetto sweatshirt over my head. "You can wear this." The tiny rattle of the unmarked bottle in my pocket made me stop short with the hood half over my head.

"Actually," I said quickly, "just help yourself to anything in my closet."

Mom raised an eyebrow at me. "You're wearing that? Out? But you have such a gorgeous figure." She stepped forward to help me out of the old sweatshirt, but I jerked away.

"It's a stipulation of Palmetto Princess," I lied. "I'm supposed to show school spirit at least three times a week." I shrugged. "One of those things no one ever tells you before you take the crown."

"Oh." My mom nodded. "In that case."

She turned to Darla, who meanwhile had slinked into the emerald mini sundress that I'd worn to our big pep rally three Thursdays ago. That was a signature piece. I was still fielding compliments for that dress, and now Darla was going to stuff her double-D boobs into it? I narrowed my eyes at her, but she just gave me that dopey open-mouth smile.

"Can I really?" she asked.

My future stepsister had me in a wardrobe headlock. I could feel Mom holding her breath for my approval.

"Of course," I finally said sweetly. "Though it really looks much better with heels. I'd lend you my snakeskin strappy sandals, but I guess your feet are a few sizes bigger. Bummer."

In the Flower Van, I slunk down in my seat as the Dick pulled out of our neighborhood. All together in the Flower Van again.

"Darla's been very affected by the news at Palmetto," he said. "She's been working on an editorial for the school paper. How are you handling it, Nat?"

The Dick's handlebar 'stache barely fit in the rearview, and I could feel him trying to catch my eye in the mirror. But there was no way I was going to let him see the deer-in-headlights look on my face. I shivered, pulled my sweatshirt tighter around me, and pretended to be absorbed by the traffic outside.

"Oh, it's awful," Mom jumped in to say. She wheeled around in the front seat to put her hand on my knee. "Natalie and Justin used to be great friends."

"You were?" Darla asked, prying her eyes off my mom's

chest brimming over the top of her shirt to look at me. Her own chest was only slightly more contained by the conservative bust of my dress.

Why did Mom have to go and say that? So what if *one* time, years ago, during a mother/daughter morning gossip session in bed, I'd spilled to Mom that I couldn't get J.B. out of my head? I'd never go around bringing up all the details of her flings in front of the Dukes. Some confidences were supposed to be a little more sacred than that.

Now I was forced to shrug. "Not really. We just ran in the same circle."

"Well, have you heard the latest about Baxter Quinn?"

My head darted from the window to look at Darla. What did she know? Was I really going to blow my cool and stoop to asking the Double D for the news?

Wait—just because I was flailing didn't mean the rest of the world was turning upside down. Here was Darla with her jutting lower lip and lack of chin, with the stringy hair that needed washing and some shine spray. She didn't know anything. Obviously, she was looking to me.

"To be honest," I said finally, "I'm pretty tired of talking about it."

Darla nodded, all apologies.

By then, the Flower Van was turning down an oak-lined avenue toward the Coveted. I knew this area well; we were heading down a ritzy alcove where Rex Freeman and Kate Richards both had weekend homes. I knew if we walked out past the bend to where the Cove dipped into a whisper-thin peninsula of pine trees, I'd be able to see Mike's house across the bay.

He didn't like the Dick any more than I did, but he was always really nice to Darla. I think he thought he was doing me a favor, but it really just bugged me to the point where I hadn't even bothered to tell him I'd be stuck with the Dukes today.

"I think you're going to like this one, Dotty," the Dick was saying, running his fingertip along the bra strap that had slid down my mother's bare upper arm. Again, he looked at me in the rearview, his mustache glinting in the sun. "Are you as picky as your mother, Nat?"

This time, I held his eyes in the mirror. "Let's just say Mom and I have very different tastes."

His eyes snapped back to the road as he pulled into a lot in front of a bright-yellow three-story house. Every house I'd ever seen in the Cove was a strict plantation-style mansion, with high white entry columns, a sprawling wraparound porch, and painted wooden shutters. To look at them all lined up along the water, you'd think keeping with that style was some sort of zoning law. But not this house. This hacienda had yellow stucco walls and a purple-and red Mexican-tiled roof. It was massive. It was heinous. It stuck out worse than a sore thumb. It stuck out the way that only new money can.

But apparently Mom disagreed. When we got out of the car and looked up at the monstrosity, she threw her arms around the Dick, cackling and kicking her legs up in the air. My mother was a buxom Julia Roberts.

"*¡Ay caramba!*" Mom giggled. The Dick's head virtually dropped into her chest when she murmured playfully, "*Mi casa es su casa, señor*"?

When they fell into a sloppy kiss, I caught Darla's eyes. For a second, my instinct was to roll mine sympathetically. After all, she might not be an A-lister at Palmetto, but the Double D was in my same boat of suffering on the shores of parental embarrassment. Why couldn't we exchange some mutual mortification?

But then, I noticed Darla looking back and forth between my mother and me—as if she were sizing us both up. She cocked her head at me and said, "Huh."

"What?"

"You have the same mannerisms as your mom. That swinging hug thing—you did that at a pep rally once."

Before I could respond to my freaky future stepsister, my matching-mannerisms mother linked her elbow through mine and started prancing with me up the path toward the house.

"Richard said," she whispered in my ear, "if we *really* like this one, he'll give it to me as an engagement present."

My mouth dropped open.

"I know," she gushed. "Which *means* . . ."

"You're actually getting married," I filled in. "Again?"

"Well, yeah." She shrugged. "But what I'm saying is—his gift, in *my* name . . . a whole house, on the good side of the Cove?" Her voice climbed up a few notes. "Don't you get it, Natalie?" She faced me and put her hands on my shoulders. "Oh, someday you will. Even if things don't work out with the Duke—"

She looked up at the Dick who was opening the upstairs balcony door.

"Did you see the swim-up bar out back, Dotty?" he called.

"Oh, *Richard*!" Mom bounded toward him, leaving me alone at the threshold of Casa de Tacky. The whole I'm-social-climbing-for-your-own-good routine was an old one with Mom. Only this time, I'd been through enough to see through it.

It was strange; Mom seemed so happy. And God knows, there'd been days when I never thought she'd get here. When my dad left town thirty-two days into my seventh-grade year at Cawdor Middle, Mom was even more desperate and lost than me. I spent most of my middle school career helping her through the rough patches in between jobs and boyfriends and bottles of wine. It got to the point where I was holding her hair back so often, I didn't have time to have problems of my own. She threw up; I grew up. By the time I transferred to Palmetto, I'd already fielded more drama than most of the girls in the senior class.

Now, here she was, four husbands later and going on her second multimillion-dollar property—purely based on her uncanny powers of feminine persuasion. My mother might be a tramp, but she was no idiot. She'd figured out her own golden secret: Security didn't come from having a man who "loved" her; it came from what those things bought her—in her own name.

I could *not* end up like this.

"Honey, come see the labyrinth," Mom called to me from the backyard.

I sighed and started trooping around the side of the house so I wouldn't have to shudder at the decor inside. But before I got to the labyrinth, I spotted Darla leaning over the balustrade talking to Kate Richards. I'd been so consumed by the god-awful hacienda, I hadn't even noticed we were just two houses down from her family's lake house.

I was just about to round the magnolia tree when I heard Darla's voice.

"It was Nat's idea that I borrow the dress," she lied, smoothing over the fabric where it puckered at her heaving chest. "Our parents are *together*."

"Nat Hargrove's mom and your dad?" Kate asked with a tiny throaty laugh. It bugged me that she suddenly sounded so interested. "And you're moving in next door? Is Nat here with you today?"

Darla nodded. "But don't bring up Baxter or J.B. or anything. It's, like, *all* people are talking to her about," she said, nodding knowingly. "Since she's Princess. She's kind of over it—"

"Oh, hi, Kate," I said, coming up on them from behind. Her Rapunzel hair was mounted in a messy bun on top of her head. Where her white wifebeater tank top cleared her jeans, I could see the pink heart tattoo on her hip. "Any word from Baxter?" I asked.

Kate raised an eyebrow at Darla, then turned to me.

"Actually," she breathed. "He finally got in touch."

Fighting the urge to seize on her for details, I calmly hoisted myself on the balcony and drawled, "Oh yeah?"

Kate leaned in. "He apologized for disappearing. He said we'll probably have dinner or something soon."

Her voice carried the unmistakable female urgency to deliver the news—and to be consoled that it was good news. I sighed. This wasn't strong-willed, fly-by-the-seat-of-her-miniskirt Kate that I'd befriended last year. You think you know a girl—and then she goes and loses her virginity at a Mardi Gras party and goes soft.

"That's great, sweetie," I cooed. "And did he mention anything about the night he disappeared?"

Kate bobbed her head. "He swears he's innocent. He says

he'll prove it soon, but he wouldn't tell me where he's been or when he's coming back."

"But . . . so he is coming back?" I asked.

I could see from the way she was looking at me, forehead creased and eager eyes, that Kate was in pretty deep. I felt for her, I did. No girl dreams of her crush disappearing immediately after her first time. But this girl really needed to snap out of it. On his best day, Baxter didn't come anywhere near deserving her. Plus, I needed a clearheaded and unemotional source of information on his whereabouts.

If I knew Baxter, wherever he was, he was probably planning on making a grand reentrance as soon as the opportunity arose. If he was already putting out teasers of his innocence and claiming to have proof, that grand reentrance sounded less than promising for Mike and me.

Maybe this wasn't going to be as simple as I'd thought. I could feel my heart start clamoring in my chest, but the only thing to do was channel that energy into something productive.

"You must be so worried," I cooed, shaking my head, "to not have any idea how to help him. If only you knew where he was, maybe then there'd be something we could do."

"I can keep trying to find out." Kate sounded hopeful at the thought of a Baxter-related project. Darla shuffled her feet.

I brushed a loose strand of Kate's hair behind her ear. "Whatever happens, you know I'll be happy to help," I said sweetly. "Just keep me posted. Anything you find out, anything you need, come talk to me."

"Of course," Kate nodded. "Thanks."

"Girls," the Dick called from the upstairs balcony, "come on up and get the tour."

Both he and my mom looked flushed. I didn't even want to think about what they'd been doing in the master bedroom. Usually, whenever I thought about other people getting it on, I'd get a flash of Mike's body over mine in bed, followed by a tingly feeling inside. Mike and I called it the flash 'n' tingle.

But today, something was different. When my mind flashed to Mike's eyes, they didn't look turned on. They looked terrified.

If I wanted to see the desire in Mike's eyes, not the fear, I needed to keep the two of us and our crowns in the clear. When I looked at Kate, I couldn't stop thinking about Baxter. Mike and I were helpless until we knew enough about what the old druggie had up his sleeve. Only then would we be able to thwart him.

CHAPTER *Twelve*

SOUND AND FURY

By Monday morning, the rumors were spreading like wildfire. The school-wide gossip circuit was another long-standing tradition at Palmetto. At the start of the week, anyone with news (loosely defined and ranging from "X made out with Y" to "Guess who spent the night in jail again") passed it around on a slip of paper—bonus points for pithy creativity. The fun was in seeing how far word could travel by the end of the day—and how screwed up it could get. Since anyone could add to or revise the news that churned, the rumor mill was kind of like the love child of Wikipedia and a game of "telephone."

No one knew who started the mill, or when, or why by now we hadn't updated the old-fashioned note-passing format to accommodate any range of technological advances. But every kid in this school loved it (and occasionally loved to hate it). So despite the loathing faculty's tired attempts to eradicate it, my guess was that the rumor mill would outlast us all.

I hadn't exactly expected to spend my first official day as Palmetto Princess mitigating rumors that had to do with me, but there I was in first period European history, censoring the notes that came around.

True or false: Princess Nat and the Double D are soon to bunk up bayside?

Someone had drawn an arrow under Darla's name and written:

So that's why real estate prices are sagging in the Coveted.

My instinct was to put a big red circle around False and forge in someone else's hand: *Premature rumoring. Paperwork not finalized so the deal could still fall through. Someone churned too soon.*

Instead, I kept my cool:

Nota Bene: There will be no Double D. The Duke's "gift" is for Hargrove use only. Anyone who wants an invite to my parties will keep this truth in mind. —NH

By next period, in French class, the second note milled through:

Rumor has it Baxter Quinn won't take these murderous little accusations lying down. He's got an alibi and a suspect of his own.

I laid the note down on the middle of my desk and tried to read anyone else's handwriting into it other than Kate's. But the telltale hot-pink pen and half-print/half-cursive writing style was unmistakable. I covertly popped a piece of Juicy Fruit and grit my teeth around its juice. I leaned down to stare at the odious note until the letters went out of focus and I could think again.

Something about my close friend relaying Baxter's Bin Laden-style communication to the whole school felt so subversive. Especially after the little conversation she and I had had at the Cove yesterday. I thought I'd made myself very clear that the lines of Baxter communication between the two of us should be kept open at all times. What became of Baxter was not for the whole school to concern themselves with.

I didn't realize I'd been bearing down so hard on my pen until a big black blob of ink started to bleed through the center of Kate's note.

Okay, so she was trying to stand by her man—fine. The real issue was how this news might grow as more people saw the note. At least I'd gotten it early enough in its infancy that I could still shape its direction. All I needed to do was tone it down again—with slightly less authorship credit this time.

Since when is Baxter Quinn sober enough to take anything standing up? Forecast of his alibi: passed the eff out. Suspected suspect: pills sold by B.Q. himself earlier that night.

I folded up the note and passed it on, knowing that Kate might push back on this one. But I hoped, in the long run, she'd understand that I was really looking out for her best interests. The sooner Baxter was out of all of our lives, the better.

Fingers crossed, the biting sarcasm of my response would nip this rumor in the bud. But before I had too much time to relax after my smooth operating, the third note of the morning hit my desk.

True or false: Seems like everyone's in favor of a second interrogation by the hot new cop on the beat.

What did that even mean? I looked around to see where the note had come from, but all the other kids in my immediate vicinity had their eyes glued to the chalkboard where Madame Virge was conjugating irregular verbs. When she put down the chalk, she looked up at the clock and reached for a slip of paper on her desk.

"I have strict orders to read this prompt," she said, getting everyone's attention because of the rare break from her native tongue to say something we could actually understand. "Don't get any ideas about me speaking English after this."

As the class groaned, Madame Virge cleared her throat and read.

"'Attention: to anyone who hasn't yet met with our new police liaison, Officer Parker. You will be called to Principal Glass's office during your regular study-hall period for a brief questioning. Every student must attend.'"

Hmm. I didn't have study hall until third period, but Mike would have had it first thing in the morning. Why hadn't he texted to give me a heads-up?

"A.J.," I whispered to Amy Jane when the bell rang to dismiss us, "did you already have study hall? What's the deal with this new cop?"

Amy Jane made a pouting face and said, "Not till last period. Sucks—the word is he's hot as hell."

I chewed on my nails and ducked out of class in a huff. I wasn't going to wait to be called down to meet this new liaison officer, hot as hell or not. I rapped on Principal Glass's door just as the next bell rang.

"Come in," an unfamiliar voice called.

Through the fishbowl walls, I could see a man in uniform standing behind the principal's desk, leaning up against the bookshelf. He looked kind of like a skinnier version of Paul Rudd. When I opened the door and stepped in, the first thing I noticed was his badge, shining like it got a fresh rub of polish every day. Then my eyes traveled down to his navy slacks, which were so snug around the groin that I wondered about a dress-code violation. He had dark hair that he'd slicked up in the front, and his thick eyebrows raised when he gestured to one of the chairs in the office and said, "Have a seat. I guess you're Palmetto's Princess, Natalie Hargrove."

"Good news travels fast," I said. "I guess you're Officer Parker."

I took a seat, eyeing him to see whether he was sleazy enough to lean forward and watch as I sat down in my short gray-blue pleated skirt and crossed my legs. So he was that kind of guy.

"I saw your picture in the paper," Officer Parker explained. "I've been reading up on your school, trying to get a feel for things. You might have guessed that they hired me to get to the bottom of what happened last weekend."

I shrugged. "I hadn't given it much thought."

O.P. scratched his prominent chin. "Was Justin Balmer a friend of yours?"

"Not really," I said. "He played football with my boyfriend."

"So I hear." He looked down at his legal pad, then up at me. "And how long have you been with your boyfriend?"

"I'm not sure what that has to do with your interrogation," I said, holding his gaze. There was something both hot and cold about his hazel eyes, like driving with the windows down and the heat on in the winter.

Officer Parker came around to the other side of the desk. I could smell the musky aftershave on his face. He gave me a thin smile.

"I'm just going to get down to it, Princess," he said. "This one stinks of something fishier than a drunk kid missing a dose of pills. You may have heard that we've got a suspect linked to a movie filmed that night."

I shook my head but stiffened my grip on the armrest. This was good: The police were already using Baxter's tape as evidence.

"Of course," he continued, "that evidence alone doesn't make the case airtight. And there's one small problem with it." He licked his lips. "Any guess what that problem might be?"

"I'm not sure what you mean," I said, uncrossing and re-crossing my legs.

Officer Parker looked down at them. "You seem like a nice girl. And Baxter Quinn wasn't much of a cameraman, anyway." He chuckled, a wheezy, sleazy sound. "A few zesty indiscretions caught on film shouldn't be held against you."

I bit my lip. Oh. Shit. In all the time I'd spent brooding over Baxter and the tape, I'd managed to overlook the scintillating scene he had shot of Mike and me earlier in the night. Of course, using that tape to bring down Baxter was too good to be true. I couldn't believe that this sleazebag cop, with the all-too-knowing twinkle in his eye, had something on me now, too.

"I just wouldn't want to see your reputation go to hell so soon after you got what you wanted," O.P. said finally.

"What I wanted?" I asked. Well. How much *did* he know? I felt so powerless and so exposed, like the whole school could see my thoughts as clearly as they could see through this glass-walled room.

"The crown," he said simply.

I exhaled.

"Look," Officer Parker said. He was close enough that I could feel his breath on my cheek. "No one's using the word blackmail. Personally, I don't even see a need to use an amateur sex tape in a court of law. Unless . . ."

His hand was on my leg. I looked around. Why wasn't anyone walking by the fishbowl right now to see what a first-class sleaze this guy was?

"What do you want from me?" I hissed.

"You're in touch with the kids at Palmetto," he said, removing his hand to cross his arms over his chest. "Point me toward some other evidence to close the case, and we can pretend this footage never even existed."

"What about Baxter? What about when he comes back?"

Officer Parker held out his hands in a grand shrug. "His word against mine? This flick's official police evidence now, Princess," he said. "Some punk kid with a drug problem won't be able to do a thing about it."

He extended his hand, and when I put mine out to shake it, he brought it to his lips. "We'll be in touch, I'm sure."

I left the office wanting a shower. What if there was more on that DVD that he wasn't letting onto? What if he was just trying to see how far he'd have to go to make me crack? And what had happened when he talked to Mike?

A small snore to my left made me jump. It was Darla, the Double D, dozing on the couch outside the principal's office. She must have sensed me standing over her because she shook awake and immediately wiped some drool from the corner of her mouth. She was sporting a Palmetto sweat-shirt, almost identical to the one I'd been wearing yesterday, except in baby blue.

"Did you just get interviewed?" she stammered. "I'm supposed to go in now. I was racking my brain to jot down everything I ever knew about J.B. I want to help—I guess I dozed off."

"Ever heard the saying about letting sleeping dogs lie?" I said under my breath.

Darla's face changed. Her eyes grew cold. Before I could apologize, she sat up in her chair.

"You might be older and more popular," she said with more venom than I knew she had in her, "but I've got bigger boobs and more money."

I laughed and cocked my head at Darla.

"And I'm supposed to be jealous of you?"

Darla shrugged. "You know, there's another saying. This one's about the apple not falling far from the tree." She swiveled her head like a contestant on a seedy talk show. "You are your mother's daughter."

"Darla Duke." A secretary's head popped out of the office. "Officer Parker will see you now."

Darla stood up, but before she entered Magnum Sleaze's den, she looked over her shoulder at me.

"We can be sisters," she said, quietly enough that the secretary wouldn't hear. "Or I can treat you like the sponge you were raised to be. Your choice."

Then she was gone. If these walls weren't so transparent, I might have grabbed Darla by the hood of that sweatshirt.

But then I spotted Mike further down the hall. As I rushed toward him, I tried hard to regain my composure. He was talking to the football team, laughing and banging his helmet on the lockers. Maybe he didn't know we were on the cusp of being blackmailed and arrested. By the time I reached him, I was furious.

He took one look at my face and turned to the guys. "I'll catch up with you in the locker room, okay?" He put his arm around my waist and pulled me in. "What's up?"

"You met Sergeant Sleaze this morning. Why didn't you tell me?"

"What are you talking about?" Mike looked at me blankly.

"He's got the DVD," I said slowly.

"I know," Mike said, actually grinning. "The guys were talking about it during practice this morning. I've been dying to see you in person all day so I could tell you." He wrapped his hand around the back of my head and whispered, "It's only a matter of time before we're off the hook."

"Are you crazy?" I swatted him away. "Didn't Officer Parker jog your memory about what else is on there?"

Mike's brow furrowed and he shook his head.

"That's great," I unzipped my backpack for a piece of gum. "He didn't mention anything. So it's only me he's blackmailing."

Now Mike's face darkened, and he clenched his teeth. He curled his hand into a fist. "What did he say to you?"

"Let's just say he's more than a little bit interested in how much of my flesh Baxter captured." I chewed. I tried to push him away, but his grip was too strong for me. "Why didn't you think of that, Mike? You should have done something about the DVD. That was your end of the deal."

Now Mike dropped his hands from my waist.

"You didn't think of it either," he said, exasperated.

"Well, now it's your turn to step up and figure out how to get your hands on it," I said. "There are a few things that need to end up on the cutting room floor before anyone can take Baxter down."

"That's ridiculous, Nat, you know it," he muttered. "Who do you think I am?" He leaned in and lowered his voice. "The DVD is in police custody, and I'm supposed to magically lift it off their hands so you don't get embarrassed for showing too much skin."

"What if there's more on that DVD than just too much skin?"

"Remind me what *you've* done to help get us out of this? What was your end of the deal again?"

I crossed my arms. "I haven't had a chance to *talk to Tracy* because I was too busy being blackmailed by the cops."

"Right, I forgot, you were supposed to talk to Tracy. I hope that won't be too risky for you. Let me know what she says—if you make it out alive."

"*Mike—*"

"I'll see you after school."

By then, he was already halfway down the hall. I wasn't about to make a scene by yelling after him in front of the Bambies clustered near the Coke machines. I stormed up the stairs toward the junior bathroom. I *would* find Tracy. And Mike was going to have to do some serious groveling if he wanted to know what I learned.

"There you are," Tracy said, pushing her sapphire glasses up on her nose when I barged through the bathroom door. "Jesus, Nat, you look like shit."

"I just—" I started to say . . . I just what?

Had a blow-out fight with my boyfriend/coconspirator?

Got compared to my social-climbing mother by the biggest loser in school?

Almost cracked under the pressure of this monster secret?

"I just got hit on by our new 'police liaison,'" I finally said. "It's wigging me out pretty bad."

"Poor thing," Tracy said, gathering her braids in a thick ponytail. "I met O.P. this morning. Smokin' but slimy, right?" She guided me over to the mirror and lit some incense. "Here," she said, starting to brush my hair with her fingers, "let's calm you down."

In the mirror, still shaking, face flushed, I hardly recognized myself. I looked so tired and so old. My hair had lost its luster, and even my dark brown eyes looked dull. Had it only been a week since Palmetto judged me worthy of the crown?

"That man is an absolute slimeball," I said.

"I know," Tracy cooed. "But as much as you might hate to hear this, you have someone in common with Officer Parker."

I shook my head. "What are you talking about? Where would you have heard something like that?"

Tracy clucked her tongue. "You know I never reveal my sources." She looked thoughtful. "I guess that's the only thing I have in common with the rumor mill. Anyway, if you want to get even with O.P., all I'm saying is, an old friend might come in handy."

"I don't get it. How do I—"

The bell rang. Tracy blew out the incense and shrugged.

"I really can't say any more. Except this: Revenge is often closer than you think, and the fall is never far behind it."

CHAPTER *Thirteen*

MORE POTENT THAN THE FIRST

After school on Monday, I ducked out the fire exit toward Mike's and my spot under the bleachers. I really wasn't up for getting sideswiped by any of the numerous people I was avoiding—from Darla Duke to Officer Parker. And I definitely didn't want to see Kate. My head was still spinning from trying to make sense of Tracy's latest enigmatic prophecy. Maybe Mike would be able to shed some light.

We always tried to hook up under the bleachers for our own version of a pep rally. Usually, I let him score a touchdown before practice because, on the field, he had to play defense. But today, after I ducked under the third rusty bleacher and navigated over the puddles to our little grassy knoll, I was surprised to find that for once, Mike hadn't beaten me there.

We didn't like to go to class angry, and we never stayed

mad past the last bell. I just assumed that both of us would be racing from eighth period toward the bleachers to make up. Now I wondered whether our argument in the halls still hadn't blown over for him. I reached for my phone to text him, but something made me hesitate. He'd either show up, or he wouldn't. And if he didn't, I thought, spitting out my gum in the grass, at least I'd know that he was really mad. Which had never happened in the whole history of Nat and Mike.

I waited, peeping out at the field from under the bleachers, and remembered a couple times this year when Mike and I had been mid-makeout, and I'd opened my eyes and strained my head to catch a glimpse of J.B. running laps around the track.

I know it was a weird thing to do, but it had always made me feel good—to know that finally, I was with the right guy. But now, the memory just made me feel sick and alone. I'd never get that same feeling again, never see the pulsing sinew of J.B.'s calves or the blond flop of his hair rustle in the wind as he ran. More than ever, I wanted Mike in my arms to take some of that pain away. I couldn't let him slip through my fingers, too.

Then, there he was, jogging out of the locker room with the rest of the guys. I felt a sharp sting in my chest. He'd ditched me. Hadn't even tried to call. And when the team made their first lap around the track, Mike looked the other way when he passed our hiding spot beneath the bleachers.

My cheeks flushed with anger. Part of me wanted to run out there and let him know that he couldn't just make an executive decision to blow me off like that. We were a team—even when things got tough, the bond we shared still had to remain sacred.

But this wasn't the time or place to bring that up, and I still had the big project of Tracy's prophecy to unfold—on my own.

I couldn't shake the memory of the vile O.P. running his hand along my leg, but it wasn't only him I needed revenge against. Baxter and O.P. were connected for me now; neither one would fall without the other. And what had Tracy meant by an "old friend" who knew Officer Parker? I scrolled through my cell phone rolodex for answers, hovered over Kate Richards' name . . . but kept scrolling. I didn't stop until almost at the end of the alphabet.

Sarah Lutsky. My old best friend from Cawdor. I was surprised that I even still had her number. Well, she *had* always had a thing for men in uniforms. But could Tracy have meant *that* old of a friend?

There was only one place to find Sarah Lutsky—that is, assuming some fundamentals of the planet hadn't changed. Within minutes, I was starting up my car and driving east. I drove across the train tracks and soon found myself back in a part of town I'd once thought I'd never set foot in again.

Other kids from Palmetto went over to Cawdor occasionally when they needed a dive-bar fix. Whenever my friends decided to go slumming, I'd always make up some emergency family excuse. The thought of those particular two worlds colliding was more than I could stand.

Today, I went in search of one old friend, in the place where I'd likely find another: my old BFF, cheap booze. Mike, of course, hated when I drank before the country-club-approved cocktail hour, but by abandoning me under the bleachers, he wasn't really leaving me much choice.

I drove past the strip of bars on Cawdor Street, recalling the years when I'd definitely patronized them a few too many times. Slowing down to find a parking spot was quite a trip down black-out lane. There was the old brothel-turned-dive-bar that probably had a few of my lacier training bras still hanging from the chandelier. There was the Mexican taco stand where I'd turned twenty-one at least twenty-one times because on your birthday, the tequila flowed freely for free. There was my favorite punk rock club—wait, where was my favorite punk rock club?

My ex-favorite haunt had a new sign, new paint job . . . and a new name.

A shiver went down my spine as I parked my car in front of the club that was now called . . . Sweet Revenge. Perhaps there was more to Tracy's prophecy than I'd guessed.

I pushed my way through the old Western-style doors and entered the bar. It was smoky inside, but when my eyes adjusted to the dimness, I could tell not much had changed. Suddenly, I was thirteen again, standing in the back corner by the pay phone, teasing guys two times my age, and taking charity Jagerbombs from my friends. You know you're too young to be drinking when a place like *this* won't even serve you. Back then, I'd had the kind of friends who'd give any rational mother an ulcer—that is, if said mother wasn't too busy being passed out on the couch.

This time, I took a seat at the bar, feeling bold from all that I'd been through in the four years since I'd set foot in this place—first the big house, then the fast car, the hot boyfriend, the sparkling crown, oh, and that one freak homicide. . . .

I shivered and pulled my jacket tighter around me.

"What can I get for you?" the bartender asked, scooting a cocktail napkin in front of me.

"SoCo and lime," I said. "Make it a double."

The drink arrived and I swallowed it down, forgetting that it was bad luck in the South not to toast to anything, even when you were alone. It just tasted so good to drink it fast. Slamming the glass down, I winced and shook my head.

"Keep them coming," I called to the bartender.

"I had a feeling you'd be back," a high, tinny voice called out.

There she was. I figured I'd have time for at least one round before Sarah got off her shift at the bowling alley. But when I looked down the bar, she was perched on the corner stool. From the looks of the row of empties in front of her, she had been sitting there since I walked through the door. Her wavy strawberry-blonde hair hung down over her tank top, and her hazel eyes were smudged with charcoal liner. Her long, narrow fingers peeled at the label on her beer, and when she smiled at me, I saw the tiniest gap between her two front teeth.

"Sarah," I said, more and more amazed by Tracy's prescience. "I can't believe it."

"Believe it," she said, standing up to slide closer to me. "People don't disappear completely just because you cut them off, Tal."

The old nickname rattled me. No one had called me that in years, not since Sarah and I had been inseparable, not since I was a Cawdor Kid, instead of a Palmetto Princess.

"And, yes," she nodded. "I heard what happened to him." She put her drink down and scooped her hair into a low ponytail. "Are you okay?"

"Fine," I said quickly. "How'd you hear?"

She looked around the empty bar and cupped my elbow. "Maybe we should grab a booth in the back," she said. "To talk."

I followed Sarah to the back of the bar, a walk we'd done many times. For a second, it felt like I was still Tal and she was still Slutsky, with her tight jeans casing her stick-straight legs and her thin tank top showing goose bumps on her arms. Slutsky was always freezing, which is why we used to joke that she needed so much warming up from the guys who hung around us.

"Hey, Slutsky," a rakish guy called from the pool table.

"Not now," she said with her same old snap. She nudged me into a dark corner booth, slid out her flask, and took a swig.

"So, I'm seeing someone new," she said.

"That's . . . good," I stammered. If she went on to say what I was hoping she'd go on to say, I was going to have to take out stock in Tracy Lampert.

"I mention it because the person I'm seeing might be of interest to you."

"I'm all ears."

"Derek Parker," she said, smirking suddenly. "You might know him by his uniform?"

"You're dating Officer Parker?" I chuckled, trying to sound as shocked as I felt excited.

"Dating? You could call it that," she said, waving her hand dismissively. "He's married, so that might not be the exact term."

In the old days, I'd say, "Slutsky, EW!" and we'd fall over ourselves, laughing about how it was kind of nasty but also kind of hot. And she'd go into more graphic detail than I even understood. But now . . .

"I can see you judging me even though your mouth is shut."

She sighed and lit a cigarette, offering me the pack. I shook my head. She shrugged again.

"The point is," she continued, "I've moved on from the old days just like you. Maybe now we can be friends again."

"How do you know I've moved on?" It wasn't exactly easy to keep up with the news from the other side of town.

"Ahh." Slutsky rubbed her hands together and smirked. "Now we're getting to the good stuff," she said. "Let's just say there are certain advantages to sucking off the law. Like . . . official police evidence?"

My mouth dropped open. "You watched that DVD?"

Slutsky nodded. "I have to say, Tal, I'm impressed. Usually when people cross over to nouveau riche, they get even more uptight, but this new guy—what's his name? He's really loosened you right up."

"You're lying." My hands gripped my glass to keep still. "Why would you, why would he—"

"Mostly for research purposes," she said. "Derek and I dabble in film a little bit ourselves. He thought we might get inspired—"

"That is so illegal and so sick."

"Chill out," she said. "You weren't half bad to watch. Nothing I haven't tried before but—"

"Slutsky," I said slowly, "do you still have the DVD? I mean—"

"Yeah, right." She shook her head. "That thing's on lock-down at the station." She blew a ring of smoke, raised her flask again, and took another long swig.

That was the thing about Sarah: She was always up for a good time, but when push came to shove, you could never really trust her to bail you out. There was no way she could understand why my reputation at Palmetto depended on that tape NOT getting out.

Maybe Tracy Lampert had been wrong, and this whole cross to Cawdor had been a waste of time. Why force me back in contact with this "old friend" if it was just going to be the same old shit? And why was Slutsky rooting through my purse? She used to do that all the time, but now, it felt really invasive.

"What are you doing?"

"Your phone's ringing," she said, fishing it out. "Ooooh." She looked at the caller ID. "Who's Mike?" she sang. "Is he the boy?"

I grabbed the phone from her and stared at Mike's number on the screen, waiting for the call to go to voice mail. I was relieved to see him calling, but there'd be no way to explain to him what I was doing in Cawdor right now.

"What was that all about?" Slutsky asked. "Trouble in paradise?"

I squinted at her, shocked to realize that it had been so long since we'd spoken, she didn't know anything about who I was anymore. There was no way and no reason to catch her up. The last time I'd talked to Slutsky, the biggest guy issue in my life had been my newly incarcerated father. I remembered the final fight we'd had, when Sarah had the nerve to take my father's side, like she was his friend over mine.

Wait a minute. Maybe I was barking up the wrong tree altogether. Was it possible that the old friend Tracy had suggested was . . . my father? On a good day, Dad had always been more of an old buddy-type than any sort of authority figure. On a bad day, well, those were the scars keeping me from getting back in touch with him. Until now.

The thing was, my father did have his connections—ethical or not. Maybe he was the only one who could help me now.

Or maybe I was crazy to believe anything Tracy Lampert said. Maybe I was really losing it.

"Hey," I said to Slutsky, making a show of looking at my watch. "I should probably take off."

Sarah looked around the bar. "Too many old ghosts for you here, huh?" she asked. "Okay, I'll walk you out."

I downed the rest of my SoCo and followed Slutsky's lead out the creaky back door of the bar. We walked through the gravel parking lot, both taking in the difference in pitch between the bustling bar and the quiet night outside. In the darkest corner of the back lot, Slutsky pointed toward a camper van with a dim kerosene lamp hanging from it.

"I'm just going to make a quick stop by the trading post," Slutsky said. "You want to come?"

"Trading post?" I asked, confused. It didn't look like the kind of place where I'd want to trade anything.

"Oh, Tal," she said, shaking her head, "you've been away too long. They've got everything, speed, Oxy—what's your poison these days?"

One of the guys was leaning up against the camper, watching us. He had a braided beard and a spiked choker. His arms were tattooed from his shoulders to his fingers.

"I think I'm just going to go," I said quietly. "Be careful, okay?"

Slutsky nodded, as if she'd already read a script of my lines. "Of course," she shrugged, leaning in to kiss my cheek. "I'll call you?"

From my car, I could see her silhouette climbing into the back of the trading post camper. I was glad to be out of there, but unsettled by the fact that I knew my next stop had to be my father's.

I decided to sleep on it before I made any impulsive moves and put the car in drive. Suddenly, I was very aware of the leather interior, surround-sound stereo system, and blinging hubcaps. Here I was, stuck in my past, sticking out because of my present.

And speaking of my present, I still hadn't listened to Mike's message:

"Don't know if you were waiting in our spot today, but if you were, I'm sorry. I just needed a little bit of time to clear my head. Don't be mad, okay? Just call me. I love you."

I sighed and tossed the phone back in my bag—but when I did, I noticed something conspicuously missing. The rattle of the bottle of pills. I quickly sifted through my backpack. Where were they?

I knew I'd had the bottle when I walked into the bar; I'd felt for it when I paid for my drinks. I replayed the last hour in my mind and remembered Slutsky rifling through my bag. That little bitch had stolen my pills! And now she was selling them at that sleazy trading post!

I almost slammed on the brakes and turned the car around. But then, a calm settled over me. Slutsky had just unwittingly done me a favor by taking away the baggage I hadn't known how to lose.

Let her have them. Now I could only hope that they'd disappeared for good.

CHAPTER *Fourteen*

A BATTLE LOST AND WON

When I woke up, everything was just as it had been before: my thin pea green comforter wrapped around me; the sun peeking through the wide east window, my father passed out on the easy chair in the living room of the trailer, where I slept on the foldout bed. I was groggy, half asleep.

"Dad?" I said. My voice had an underwater slowness to it. "I'll make some coffee, okay?"

Silence from the chair. Dad's arms were thrown up over his head in slack fists, and his cheeks were bristly and bloated. He'd kicked off one shoe by the door, but the other one still hung from his foot at an odd angle, like it had been twisted. A spider inched along the back of his headrest. He was so gruesome; I couldn't stop staring at him. It seemed like lifetimes since I'd seen him, but then, it was just another day. Wasn't it?

I stood over him, shaking his shoulder. "Dad," I said more loudly. Then my heart picked up, and I turned towards the back of the trailer. "Mom!"

In the bedroom down the short hall of the trailer, I waited for my mother's moan and rustle in the bed. We had a whole routine: I'd call again; she'd gripe her way to the door and stick her bed head out into the hallway—sometimes with a backward glance toward the bed. She could have anyone in there—anyone willing to sneak out between the time I left for school and whenever my dad came to.

"Mom," I called again. "He's really out this time."

Suddenly, Dad's fingers clamped around my wrist. I looked down, and his eyes snapped open.

"Shut your mouth. Nobody's out."

I screamed because he'd scared me, because his grip was tight and his breath smelled dead, because his lips and his gums were blue.

"Mom?" I called again. My voice wobbled through the cramped room.

"Your mom's not here," he spit. "She didn't bother coming home last night."

"How would you know?" I said, wrestling free to scurry to the corner of my bed.

It was then that Dad lurched from the easy chair and came at me. I didn't think he had it in him to make it across the trailer, but then again, when he wanted to scare me, it didn't matter how strung out he was.

"You think I don't know what goes on in my own house?"

When he stood up fully, which was rare, Dad was the height of the trailer's low ceiling. His big arm reached for one of the bottles of painkillers strewn across the kitchen table, but he stopped to look up at me. I could feel my lips trembling. I was willing him to inhale his morning fistful. It'd be better for us both if he just swallowed them down.

"I know what your mom tells you," he said in a low voice. "Talking behind my back as if I'm half a man. You think I need it?" He'd uncapped the bottle, but instead of taking out the pills, he chucked the whole thing at me, hard. The bottle bounced off my thigh, and the pills clattered across the floor.

"You think I need any of you?" he yelled.

"Dad," I pleaded, wincing when he pinned me up against the wall. His fist came close to grabbing my hair, but when I ducked to dodge him, he stumbled forward, knocking his shin on the bed.

"Damn it, Tal," he groaned, grabbing his leg and hopping on one foot toward his chair.

I grabbed my purple backpack and shoved flip-flops on my feet, not caring that this meant I was going to school in my pajamas, again. Better to show up in flannel pants today than covered in bruises tomorrow.

"You get back here," Dad yelled, chasing me out into the yard of the trailer park.

I kept running. I only looked back when I heard the thud.

My father was face first in the dirt. It wasn't the first time he'd fallen like that, but it was the first time I'd seen him lie there silently, not trying to get up. He'd tripped over the bottom step of the trailer and come down hard. I saw the smear of blood dripping from his lower lip. His eyelids fluttered and he was out again. I reached down to his neck, felt his pulse, then turned around and kept on running.

Mom showed up at school that day to tell me that the cops had picked him up. It was the last time either of us saw him. It was the first time I started keeping that old promise never to speak to him again.

Could a man change? Definitely not.

He opened the door before I'd even finished knocking. He looked frail and tired; the skin around his silver eyes looked loose like a grandfather's. But when he put out his arms, they were unexpectedly steady.

"Tal-doll," he said, waiting for a hug.

I stood on the metal steps of my Uncle Lewey's trailer, my arms crossed tight over my waist. I was fighting the part of me that wanted badly to step toward my father and put my head on his broad chest. Instead, I stared at the point on his forehead directly between his eyes. It was an old trick I'd learned in debate class—use it when you're too nervous to look someone in the eyes but still want to display your control.

"What do you want?" I said.

"To congratulate you," he said, nudging me with his bony elbow. "My daughter the Princess. Not that I'm surprised."

"I don't need you to say congratulations."

Dad frowned. "Okay, then maybe I need you to say, 'Welcome home.' I'm still on probation, of course, but with enough good behavior, everything can go right back to—"

"No," I said, feeling the old tremble come back into my voice. "It's different now. Mom and I are different. We moved on." My voice strained with the hope that this was true.

"Come in," Dad said, ignoring me and holding open the door. "I'll make you some tea. You look beautiful, but you don't look well."

Before Dad left and Mom and I moved out, Uncle Lewey's trailer had been three doors down from ours. It was always the bachelor-party zone. I still expected to find a free-for-all of drugs and booze, maybe a woman no one knew asleep in the corner.

But when I stepped inside today, the place looked modest and clean, with two worn place mats on the table and a silk Jessamine in a small plastic vase. It smelled like disinfectant and shaving cream.

Dad's favorite photo still hung on the wall above the kitchen table. Mom had snapped it with her disposable Kodak down by the wharf. Dad, Uncle Lewey, and I stood posed in front of the famous *Caught 'er in Cawdor* billboard, reserved for the lucky fisherman who caught a fish weighing more than fifty pounds. In the picture, Uncle Lewey's arm looped proudly under the fish's head, and Dad held up its stomach. I stood at the tail end, straining even then to hold up the weight. I was six years old, and though I didn't know it, Dad was already dragging me down.

"You'll notice things have changed around here," he said today, spooning the instant Lipton powder into two mugs and topping them off with boiling water from an electric kettle on the windowsill. "I'm not the guy you remember. My buddies at the station say they hardly recognize me."

I rolled my eyes. When Dad referred to his buddies at the station, he meant the cops who took his bribes for that brief period of time after his arrest, before the embezzlement charges came out. Dad could go on for days about his buddies at the station. A lot of good they'd done him when the shit finally hit the fan. I couldn't believe he was even still speaking to them.

"What else do your buddies at the station have to say these days?" I asked, keeping my eyes on my tea.

"Oh, that's right." Dad snapped his fingers. "You're over on that side of the world now." He chuckled. "You know, when bad things happen to rich folks, everybody gets worked up. Sounds like the dead kid's old lady has this new cop on a real witch hunt."

"What do you mean?" I said. I thought Officer Parker was working for the school, not Justin's family.

"You know, the families are always happier with a closed case." He waved his mug in the air. "Understandable," he said. "But these young cops, they just want to pin the first guy on the list. The bad news is, the first guy on the list is some kid with an alibi for the night of the murder."

"Oh, yeah?" I asked, trying to sound as disdainful as possible—without completely shutting my dad down. "And did your buddies at the station entrust you with any details of that alibi?"

"Get this," Dad laughed. "The kid was in rehab. He was too busy drugging himself to drug anyone else."

I shook my head. "But Baxter's not in rehab," I said. "He was there the night of the party."

Dad nodded, like he'd heard all this before. "It was one of those middle-of-the-night deals," he explained, "where they cart the kid off while he's sleeping. Convenient that it happened the night of the accident, but . . . wait a minute—" His voice changed. "What were you doing at that party?"

"Please. You lost all your fatherly privileges years ago." I waved him off. "Who have you been talking to anyway? Officer Parker? Do they know when Baxter's going to get out?"

Dad was looking at me strangely. He took a slow sip of his tea.

"Why so interested in Baxter?" he asked. "You're not mixed up with this guy, are you, Tal?"

"I'm not mixed up in any of it," I said quickly, defensively.

Suddenly, I could see myself through his eyes. What must I look like, cheeks flushed and breath in my throat, firing off frantic questions to someone I swore I'd never speak to again?

I stood up, pushing my stool back. It was stupid to have ever thought he could help me with something like this.

"You got me worried, doll," Dad said, his head cocked to the side. "I thought you were seeing someone nice, that King boy."

"You stay away from Mike and you stay away from me," I said, walking toward the door. "You have enough on your plate, worrying about yourself."

Dad had his hands up in the air, like, "I surrender."

"I'm your father," he said. "And I love you. I'm back in your life now, and I'm straight as an arrow, I swear. You can come to me if you need anything." He reached for my arm. "Do you need anything?"

His hand on my arm was so familiar, so complicated. I hated it, but I couldn't shake myself free. How had he found his way back to me—after I'd come so far away from him?

But then, out of anyone, maybe my dad could understand how I'd gotten myself in so deep. Maybe it wouldn't be so bad to share this load with someone else. When I looked up at his silver eyes, I saw the same sparkle that I used to carry in my own. I opened my mouth to speak.

"Just tell me what you need," he said again, more softly.

It was that yearning in his voice—that need to be needed not so different from the Bambies, and I lorded it over the Bambies. My stomach turned.

Behind him, something caught my eye. A large black spider spinning a web from the ceiling of the trailer. And behind it, the neat line of liquor bottles stashed behind a box of cereal. I looked at my dad. Part of his sentence was to get sober and stay clean. Suddenly I saw that nothing had changed—nothing except for me.

I wrenched my arm free of him.

"I'm leaving," I said. "Stop calling me."

I grabbed the doorknob and thrust it open, catching a blast of cold air in my throat. I started to run. As the sound of my feet pounded the pavement, the desperate reality of my situation grew clearer and clearer.

Dad had been my last chance out. And he'd failed me yet again.

CHAPTER *Fifteen*

NIGHT'S BLACK SHADOWS

Whenever Mike and I agreed to meet at our secret spot over the Cove, the plan unfolded the same way:

Rendezvous, one of us would text in the morning, and the other would know what it meant.

Midnight, at the falls, dress darkly and go quietly.

Today, I'd been the one to send the text, feeling uncharacteristically nervous even as I used the code we'd used countless times before. The difference was that usually Mike and I just went there to relax and spend some time together. Tonight, my agenda was a little more ambitious. This whole week had been one catastrophe after another, and even as I tried to start piecing together the fragments of a plan, I knew it wouldn't feel real until I'd looped Mike in.

Okay was all he'd texted back.

When the full moon was high in the clear, dark sky and my mom had come home from her regular Wednesday night bowling date with the Dick—tipsy enough that she passed out in her clothes on top of the bed—I pulled a black turtleneck over my head and slunk out into the night.

We loved this waterfall. Mike had stumbled on it as a kid and had been coming here himself for years. He brought me here on our third date with a bottle of champagne and a picnic basket. I brought him here on his birthday and had all the props waiting to role-play Tarzan and Jane. It was the site of our first disagreement, our first time, our first anniversary. And luckily, it also was the one romantic spot in Charleston where we'd never run into another couple trying to squeeze in a covert grope. Having been there enough times by now, I was pretty sure that Mike and I were the only two people in the world who knew the secret waterfall existed at all.

To get there, you had to park at the marina across from the Isle of Palms. Then you trooped straight up a craggy washed-out trail for almost a mile before you got to the line of maple trees and a thick patch of Spanish moss hiding the waterfall. But once you waded through the fecund forest, the view was well worth all the huffing and puffing.

The falls cascaded cleanly down a limestone cliff and landed in a pool of water that, in the moonlight, was almost obscenely aquamarine. It wasn't that high—nothing in the Charleston area rose very far above sea level. But over the years, a perfect limestone niche for two had formed directly underneath the stream. On an early night like tonight, a slower stream of water from a nearby mineral spring sprayed off a cloaking mist that made being there feel kind of like being in a dream.

Every time we went to the falls, Mike arrived before me. He always left a trail from the spot where the path ended to where I'd find him under the alcove, because even though I'd been there enough times to find it in my sleep, Mike still said he didn't want to lose me on the way. He'd sprinkle rose petals or chocolates or birdseed—once he'd even left a few pairs of his boxers in the tree branches, like flags leading me right to him.

Tonight, the path was bare.

My heart raced at the thought of being stood up a third time, but when I dipped under the sheet of water to the alcove, Mike was there. He was seated on our rock with his head in his hands.

"You didn't leave me a trail," I said.

"I thought you liked doing things on your own," he said. His black shirt sagged at the shoulders, and his face looked as white as the moon. "Besides," he said sadly, "haven't we left enough trails already?"

"Mike," I said. He stood up when I went to him. We

wrapped our arms around each other and just stood there for a moment.

"I've missed you," I whispered.

"I'm sorry," he whispered back, "about the other day."

He lifted me up and I swung my legs around his waist. Then he backed me up against the wall of rocks and pressed his body against mine. We kissed. It was long and hot and very us. Something in me welled up with relief.

But when Mike pulled away, we both opened our eyes, and the unwelcome, unfamiliar fear found its way into our waterfall.

"What are we going to do?" he asked, setting me down.

"Look, I've got everything figured out," I said, leading Mike back to his seat on the rock. From my backpack, I pulled out a foil-covered plate of my specialty Carolina Bourbon Brownies that always got Mike's mind focused before a test.

"What's all this?" he asked.

"Sustenance to help us strategize," I said, popping a well-done corner piece in his mouth. "I've been thinking, just in case Baxter's DVD does prove too hard to get a hold of, we're going to need a plan B. Which is why I've found the perfect way to keep Officer Creeper in check."

"I like the sound of that," he said.

"You do?" I asked, leaning into him. Everything depended on Mike being with me on the plan.

"Are you kidding?" Mike raised an eyebrow in that sexy way of his. "After the way that guy treated you in the fishbowl the other day? I'm all ears."

"A little bird tells me Officer Parker is packing an incriminating DVD or two of his own," I said, gaining confidence as he egged me on. I wiggled my finger through his button-down shirt and tickled his ribcage. This was much more like it. "I'll get us access to proof of O.P.'s statutory ways," I said. "And if he's still not cooperating, we might just have to air his dirty laundry." I leaned in for the clincher. "During regularly scheduled 'Path to Palmetto' programming at the Ball."

Since Mike and I had more footage of the two of us over the past three years than probably any other couple, everyone was expecting our film to be of Oscar-worthy caliber. We'd finished editing it way before Palmetto had even announced the winners, so all that was left to do was turn it in to the Anger, resident dance technician, who vetted it through the fishbowl to make sure it was PG enough for the dance. I loved our movie almost as much as I loved wearing the crown.

So it gave me a sizable pang of sadness to think about pulling our tape from the deck. But when I saw the intrigued look on Mike's face, I knew it would be worth the sacrifice.

"You're going to rig the 'Path to Palmetto' segment at the Ball to play an Officer Parker sex tape?" He laughed, incredulous. "You really want to do that? But you love our movie."

"I also love the idea of blackmail for the blackmailer," I said.

"Well, that would do the trick."

I smiled. "He'll be lamer than a Carolina duck in hunting season."

Mike ran his hand through my hair. It felt so good I closed my eyes and just basked in the simple comfort of the moment. But when I opened them, his brow was furrowed yet again.

"What?" I asked, sitting up and taking his hand. "What's going on with that look?"

Mike kissed my hand, but his eyes still looked worried. "I'm glad you figured something out about O.P. I mean, I could kill that guy. But there's something I have to tell you."

I nodded.

"I have some news about Baxter," he said.

"He's in rehab," I said without looking up. "I know that."

"Yeah, well, not for long." Mike sighed. "He's on his way back, just in time for the Ball on Friday."

A rush of humid water from the fall seemed to choke me. I dropped the brownie in my hand.

"How did you hear about this?" I demanded. "Why didn't you tell me?"

"I'm telling you now." Mike sounded defensive. "I got a letter from him today. He says he knows what we're up to, Nat. I don't think he's going to let us get away with it."

"But . . . what happened was an accident," I stammered. "It wasn't our fault!"

"I know that," Mike agreed. "But what's happened since J.B., all this plotting . . ." He trailed off. "You do realize we're framing someone with murder?"

"Of course, I realize it. I've spent every waking minute consumed by it. But what other choice do we have? It's going to end up being Baxter's word against ours. Who do you think the school's going to believe?"

Mike stepped away. He was rubbing his forehead again.

"I think we're in over our heads." He bit his lip. "The letter came through Kate. I think she's got his back."

I narrowed my eyes. This was an unwanted twist. Under normal circumstances, I might have pulled Kate aside to school her on the perils of expecting too much from a guy like Baxter. I might have suggested she just cut her losses and move on. But Kate had crossed me twice now in the wrong week, when Mike and I didn't have the time or energy to look out for anyone's best interests other than our own.

"Kate is nothing more than a childish slut with too much money, and Baxter is a junkie," I huffed finally. "I guarantee you as soon as she gets distracted by another guy, she'll have no problem abandoning her post. It's not like she's getting any conjugal visits while Baxter's under house arrest."

"Okay," Mike said, "so . . ."

"So that's it." I smirked. "You get one of your linebacker friends to hit on her at the Ball. Make sure he takes her home. I guarantee, it will be like Baxter Quinn never even existed."

Mike nodded, but he was starting to look confused again.

"Hey." I cupped his chin. "Remember a short while ago when you loved my single-minded masterfulness?"

He gave a sad little laugh. "I do," he said.

"It's still me, baby. We're still in this together. I just want to stand up there next to you and wear that crown. I know you want it, too."

"I don't know," he said. His words came fast and sounded nervous. "It's like, I want to reach out and touch you, to make you feel better, to make myself feel better. That's all I know how to do." He shook his head. "But recently, I feel like I don't know anything. I love you and I'm trying, but I don't know who you are."

It was only then that I realized how disconnected Mike and I really were. We'd never had to try before. There'd never been a need to reconnect because we were always just together. Our friends even called us John and Yoko, teasing us because wherever one of us was, you could always find the other.

I reached for his belt buckle. Maybe it was a reflex. It was all I could think of to keep us together, even though part of me knew it was wrong.

"No," he said, flicking my hand away.

I looked down at my hand as if I'd just been stung. I felt my face fall. Mike had just swatted me away. He didn't mean it. He couldn't.

I sat down next to him on the rock and pulled his lips to mine. He kissed back, but something about it was like a reflex more than a desire.

This was so frustrating. I wrapped my arms around his neck and kissed harder, slipping my tongue between his teeth. I waited for the pull on my bottom lip that always told me he was really into it . . . but it never came.

After a minute, he pushed me back. My heart raced, panicked.

"I'm sorry," he said. "I just can't pretend like everything is okay. I can't push what we did out of my mind."

I sat mortified on the rock, with no part of my body touching Mike's. I felt like he'd slapped me in the face. A light breeze picked up, and I suddenly realized my face was damp. Tears were streaking down my cheeks.

"Natalie," he whispered, clearly pained—which just made it worse. I felt myself breaking, ever so slightly. Something inside me was snapping. And he still kept his hands in his lap, not touching me. "Don't." His voice broke and I began crying in earnest.

"I can't help it," I said, soaking my shirtsleeves with my tears. "I can't. . . . I just can't do this alone."

At last, he turned to me and tucked my hair behind my ear. He kissed my eyelids, getting his lips wet with my tears.

"You're not alone," he said. "I'm in this with you. You know I am." I tried to take a deep breath, but it had been so long since I had really cried that now I felt like I couldn't control it. I was so tired. So, so tired.

He brushed my hair back again with his strong hands and finally showed me the smile I hadn't realized I'd been craving all week. "Here," he said, "I have something for you."

"You do?"

I wiped my eyes while Mike reached behind him and pulled out a large white box.

"I know you've been waiting for this," he said, handing it to me.

When I opened it, I gasped. I had completely forgotten that tomorrow was Jessamine Day. I'd been waiting four years to get the all-white senior privilege flower, instead of the gaudy, colored underclassmen one. And this Jessamine was perfect. My eyes stung as fresh tears threatened—in all of this awful mess, Mike had still remembered. He still loved me. I wasn't alone.

And the Jessamine. It was gorgeous.

It was big enough to make an impression but completely tasteful in its design. I held it up to my heart, where I'd wear it pinned to my overalls to school tomorrow. The centerpiece was a crown with an opal at its center.

"I had to have it specially ordered," Mike said. "The Dick had to call three factories to find that there crown. It's the only one in the state. But I knew what I wanted," he said. "And I got it."

"It's perfect. It's royal," I said, slipping my tongue in his mouth. This time he kissed me back softly.

"Is it too heavy for you?" he asked when we pulled away for breath.

I pressed my mouth against his again, glad to feel his tug on my lower lip.

"With your help bearing the load," I said, "I think I can manage."

CHAPTER *Sixteen*

THE SERPENT UNDER THE FLOWER

"Have you seen what the Double D is wearing on her overalls today?" Jenny asked the next morning by my locker.

I snorted, adjusting my Jessamine to hang at a perfectly straight angle. "I didn't think she'd show. How'd she get a date?"

"Au contraire," Amy Jane said. Her own Jessamine was gaudy and glittering. It lit up like a Christmas tree when you pressed a button at its center. I would never wear anything close to it, but somehow Amy pulled it off. She lowered her voice and leaned in. "The D.D. is dateless. Her daddy made a Jessamine for her out of pity."

"Of course he did," said Jenny, whose Jessamine was totally old-school and tasteful, its centerpiece a rare real flower.

Jenny cleared her throat and nodded at my own Jessamine. "I'm sure that's how she got a crown as her centerpiece, too."

"What?" I gasped. "Mike said mine was the only one in the state."

Amy Jane grimaced and took out some cooling cucumber facial mist from her bag. "Uh uh uh," she coaxed. "No stressing today. You cannot get all puffy-faced before your big night tomorrow."

"*I'm* the Princess. Double D is hardly a groundling." I could feel my breath quicken, and I held on to the base of my locker for balance. Usually something like this wouldn't unnerve me so much.

"She's flipping," Jenny said. "Nat, you must stay calm. Darla's mum is tacky and looks nothing like yours—"

"Except for the crown," Amy Jane said automatically.

Both Jenny and I shot her a look. She shrugged.

"Sorry," she said. "Jenny's right—Double D's flower is school colors. Utterly tacky. Anyway, she won't even be at the dance tonight—it's not like she can get away with bringing Daddy as her date."

"Whereas you, Princess Nat," Jenny picked up, "will be the belle of the Ball" —she looked at her watch—"in less than twenty-seven hours. At least if I have anything to do with it." She clapped her hands and opened her PDA. "Now we're all meeting tomorrow at four o'clock with garment bags and cosmetics, yes?" Amy Jane and I nodded. "The Bambies are coming to help—don't groan, you know they're good at the grunt work—"

"At least that's what the football team says. . . ."

Jenny rolled her eyes at Amy Jane. "Nat, you gave Ari Ang the DVD of your 'Path to Palmetto' story?"

"Of course," I said, my heart fluttering briefly about the alternate DVD I had tucked in my backpack and what I was about to undo. Slutsky had come in handy after all. Once I'd called her out on the pills she'd picked out of my purse, she'd been more than happy to "lend" me a naughty tape of her and Officer Parker for sex education purposes only, of course.

"Oooh, I can't wait," Jenny squealed. "I bet it's the best 'Path to Palmetto' this school has ever seen."

I beamed at her and nodded. It was certainly going to be memorable. And more importantly, after tomorrow night, Officer Parker wouldn't be giving me any more problems. Now all I had to do was find a minute today to sneak into Ari Ang's projector room and swap the tapes.

The bell rang, and the girls and I exchanged hugs.

"Happy Jessamine Day," we called on our way to class.

En route to French, I knew I'd find Mike by his locker. I snuck up behind him and covered his eyes with my hands. He jumped and turned around, then tried to recover and look relaxed when he saw that it was me.

"Sorry," he said. "Don't know why that scared me." He looked down at the Jessamine, and his old grin spread across his face. "Hey . . . *nice* bud. I've been listening to people sing the praises of that Jessamine all day. Now I see why. You wear it so well."

He swooped me up, smashing the Jessamine a little in the process, but I didn't even care. I sucked playfully on his neck and purred.

"I'm so glad things are back to perfect with us," I said.

"Hate to interrupt," a voice called from behind us. We broke our embrace to find Officer Parker, with his eyebrows raised and his hands on his hips. "But I'm afraid I'm going to have to ask you to keep it clean in the hallway." He shook his head at me. "And I thought you might have learned a lesson from our conversation last week. Maybe you're just too much of a little sl—"

"You shut your mouth." Mike's fist was clenched, and I knew it was on its way around Officer Parker's collar.

"Mike," I jumped in, pushing them apart. "Stop it," I gasped. "He's right. Let's just go to class."

I hauled him toward our last class, and we left O.P. fuming in the hallway.

"Don't worry, baby." I grabbed Mike's hand. "He won't be on our backs for long."

But instead of heading to my French class, I dropped Mike off at his history class and waited until the halls were clear.

Then I slipped into the A/V room with the DVD burning in my bag.

The windowless studio was dark and cold, and I bumped into more than a few rolling TV stands before I found a desk lamp. I'd only taken one media class at Palmetto, my first semester here, but from the looks of the same rickety tape reels, torn projector screen, and mystifying PA system, you'd think not much had changed in the world of technology over the past three years. I waded past the dated electronics toward the attic, an alcove jutting over the back of the gymnasium. Tomorrow night, Ari Ang would emcee the dance from here.

The Anger was nothing if not organized, so it shouldn't be too difficult to find his neatly labeled multimedia binder for the Ball. I'd already labeled my replacement DVD with the same Mike 'n' Nat sticker that decorated the real "Path to Palmetto" DVD, so everything was ready to go.

I pulled open the thick soundproof door to the attic and stepped in. The room was a myriad of knobs and blinking lights that I would never understand, but it did have one of the best aerial views in the school. The tinted window above the main control panel overlooked the gym, which overlooked the football field, where we'd all had so many good memories.

But when I leaned up against the glass to look out, I was

struck by one specific memory, the kind of memory I was least expecting.

I'd spent the bulk of first semester freshman year working on my final project for Media 101, a documentary on the town of Charleston. I remember being surprised to find myself so into it—maybe all those hours cutting footage in the A/V room were an excuse to be away from Mom and her sugar daddy du jour. But in the end, I remember being really proud of it. I was watching the final cut after school one day in the alcove when Justin Balmer barged in unannounced.

I'd had the soundproof headphones on, so I didn't hear anything until he tapped me on the shoulder. I'd spun around so fast I knocked them off.

"Whoops," he sounded surprised. "I was looking for Amber. Sorry."

Amber Lochlan was a cool older girl in my media class, who went on to be that year's Palmetto Princess. She had the same short dark hair as I did, so maybe we could have passed for each other from behind. But I liked to think my hair was not as susceptible to humidity as Amber's.

I shrugged at J.B. "Haven't seen her."

"Hey, wait a minute," he said, pointing his finger at me. "I know you."

I froze, trying to shake my head that no, he didn't. I wasn't anyone he knew.

A smile spread across his lips. "You're the new girl who keeps avoiding me. Which makes you my next target."

"You should save yourself the trouble," I said, fumbling to pull my headset back on. "It's not going to happen."

"Ouch . . . so harsh." He leaned forward, almost grazing my lips with his. "I swear we knew each other in another life. You should give me another chance."

My body tingled at his touch, but my mind recoiled at his nerve. After a few panting breaths, I forced myself to push him away.

"Never," I spit, not letting myself make the mistake of tacking on the word *again*.

J.B. squinted at me then, and I hung there, terrified, after vowing how many times that I would never let myself feel trapped by a guy again.

And then what I remember most was the way his expression changed in that moment. The color drained from his face, and the side of his mouth started quivering. His eyes widened, like he was afraid, but then just as quickly, they narrowed into slits. He said nothing, just barged back out the attic door with awkward lurching steps that I'd chalked up to too much testosterone.

Now, three years later, alone in the attic again, I shivered. I'd been too consumed by my own fear that day to see what was behind his hasty exit. J.B. must have needed his meds, even back then. He must have been swallowing down those Trileptal as soon as he was out of eyeshot, while I struggled in my own way to compose myself over the control panel.

I yanked open the file cabinet. I *had* to stop letting him haunt me. I was going to make it through tomorrow night. And it wouldn't be a good start to get busted lurking around the A/V room. Rifling through the file folders, I found Ari's materials for tomorrow night. Inside the green tabbed folder were playlists for slow songs, playlists for fast songs, scripts for the faculty speakers. And our "Path to Palmetto" DVD.

This was no time for sentimental flip-flopping. I couldn't think about the opening shot of the two of us walking arm in arm on Capers Beach. I swapped the CDs, slipped the original in my backpack, and headed for the door.

The bell for second period was about to ring, and I could still make it into my English class without incident. Tumbling back out into the brightness of the hallway, I turned the corner and nearly had a heart attack when I ran smack into Kate.

"What are you doing here?" I blurted.

"It's called a hall pass." She waved the laminated card in my face. "What's your excuse?" Her eyes narrowed at me. "Why so on edge, Princess?"

There was a new iciness in her voice that I didn't like the sound of. Had she seen me come out of the A/V room?

"Love your Jessamine." I changed the subject swiftly, tugging on a particularly garish purple bell attached to her flower. "Did Baxter get it for you?"

"Mmm . . . more or less," she stuttered. "He was able to call in the order absentee. I went to pick it up from the Duke last night—" She broke off, then looked up at me coolly. "You know what, I don't need to justify this to you. You've made it more than clear what you think of him."

I looked at the pride with which she wore that kitschy Jessamine and sighed. Mike and I had enough on our hands, what with taking the throne *and* taking down Baxter and O.P. We could not afford to have Kate cross over to the other side, too.

"Kate," I cooed, cupping her cheek, "can't you see, all I want is for you to be happy? And . . . if a long-distance rehab relationship spells happiness for you . . . well, who am I to judge?" I smiled, squeezing her shoulder in good-bye. "See you tomorrow night."

CHAPTER *Seventeen*

OUT DAMN SPOTLIGHT

"May I present," Jenny read from her prompt into the microphone in front of the whole student body, "the Prince and Princess of Palmetto—Mike King and Natalie Hargrove!"

It was three hours later, and I was made-up and poured into my long plum-colored gown, standing hand in hand with Mike behind the curtain separating us from our subjects. Both of us wore our glittering crowns. I could feel the energy of the whole school on the other side of the curtain. When it rose, the crowd would roar, and Mike would escort me down the stage for our private waltz, the kick-off dance of the party. I couldn't wait to get out there.

I knew my Jessamine sat in a glass cage under a spotlight on the stage so the rest of the school could come up and admire it more closely. I also knew that in a video projector at the back of the room, the very surprising DVD lay waiting for its premiere.

"You ready, baby?" Mike squeezed my hand.

"I've been ready for so long," I said.

A drum roll rose up from the orchestra pit, and the glittering purple curtain rose up in front of us. Mike and I blinked into the bright lights shining down on us. I held my breath. The gym was packed with everyone we knew, transformed into the best-looking versions of themselves. Thick drapes of pearls covered the ceiling, giving the whole place the feel of an opalescent tent. The music for the classic Palmetto waltz began, and Mike turned to me and grinned.

"May I have this dance?" he asked.

We'd gone over the routine a hundred times before—in Mike's bedroom, in the halls at school, under the bleachers as foreplay. But when we started dancing, I realized that we hadn't practiced once since everything happened with J.B. For a moment, both of us seemed to remember this at the same time, and we looked at each other a little bit terrified. But then, amazingly, the steps came right back to us both, as naturally as if we'd been rehearsing around the clock all week. The lights were so bright I couldn't see anyone in the crowd, but I could imagine all of their faces, upturned and smiling at our first dance.

"Let's hear it for the royal couple," Jenny emceed when the song came to a close. The applause was loud and passionate. "Now, I invite you all to come out to the dance floor and *get on down*."

Mike swung me around in one final lift and dipped me back for a kiss.

"Drinks?" he said.

"Drinks."

We scooted to the back of the room where the massive bowls of virgin lunch-lady-made punch were being customarily spiked by Rex Freeman's team of JV protégés.

"This is quite an operation, Rex," I laughed.

He shrugged. His flushed face was as red as his hair. "I can't do all the work myself," he said. "How about two royally strong ones for the Prince and Princess?" he called to his workers.

The drinks were delivered, and Mike and I sat on a tall booth looking out at the party spinning before us. Everyone looked incredible—big hair and bold colors for the girls. The guys wore classy tuxes with handkerchiefs matching the color of their dates' dresses.

"We needed this, didn't we?" Rex said, with a rare tone of sincerity in his voice. "I mean, after the week we've all had, we all needed to just let loose."

Mike and I looked at each other and nodded.

Rex clapped us both on the shoulder. "It's you guys who are making things right again. Another Prince and Princess might have lost it. You two kept everyone strong this week."

"Thanks, man," Mike said, putting his hand over Rex's, but keeping his eyes on me. Rex looked down and shuffled his feet. When he looked back up, he'd lost his serious look and had his usual lecherous gleam in his eyes.

"Well, I feel like a pud now," he said. "I'm going to go get in touch with myself again by breaking off a piece of that Bambi over there."

When he was gone, I leaned my head on Mike's shoulder. He was laughing.

"Take a look at what's happening on the dance floor. All my hard work is paying off."

I followed Mike's pointer finger and spotted Kate, in a pink cocktail dress, mugging down with a tall dark-haired and anonymous football player.

"Who is that?" I asked.

"Who cares," Mike said. "It's not Baxter Quinn. Rex told me Baxter had the nerve to show up tonight—"

"*What?*" I gasped.

"Don't worry," Mike rubbed my neck. "He never even made it through the doors. Apparently he reeked of whiskey, and Glass sent him right back to his parole officer." He pointed back out at the dance floor where the linebacker was grinding up on Kate. "Looks like that dude is definitely going to get the job done tonight."

Everything was falling into place. Even though Officer Parker was keeping busy separating kids who were getting too freaky on the dance floor, at least he was giving us some space.

Before we knew it, Mike and I were being called back up to the stage where the dance committee had wheeled out two thrones for us to sit on while everyone watched our "Path to Palmetto" footage . . . or so they thought.

Principal Glass took the stage.

"Just a quick word," he droned.

"Yeah, right!" someone hooted from the dance floor.

"To congratulate the student body," Glass continued obliviously, "on your maturity and grace in the face of such a difficult week."

"I'll show you grace, asshole," the hooter shouted again.

Whoa. I was all for taking little jabs at how lame Principal Glass was, but I was surprised that someone would be this ballsy about it. I tried to think of who would have the nerve. . . . Baxter Quinn *better* not have weaseled his way back in here.

Why didn't Glass stop to quiet the crowd?

"I know that all of us will continue to deal in our own ways with the loss of Justin Balmer. He is in our hearts and minds every day."

"I call *bullshit* on that!"

Wait a minute, I recognized that voice. Slightly boyish with just a hint of a twang. But no, that was impossible. I looked over at Mike to see whether he was thinking the same thing I was thinking. He looked back at me and smiled. Didn't he hear it?

"I want to thank the entire student body for cooperating so fully with our wonderful Officer Parker," Glass said.

"Anyone had a full cavity search yet?" the voice in the audience leered.

I stood up from my throne and stepped forward on the stage. I had to figure out where it was coming from.

"Nat," Mike whispered. "Sit down. What are you doing?"

"I have to find him," I whispered back.

"I don't think now's the time. We can deal with O.P. later."

"Not O.P.," I said. "That voice . . . it's—"

J.B.

Feverishly, I stumbled backward, hitting the ground on all fours, just in front of the throne. Justin was walking toward us, but his feet weren't touching the ground. Instead, his steps moved slowly over the heads of the rest of the students. It was like he was lit up from inside. And he looked so sexy in his tux. There was a handkerchief tucked in his lapel—the same deep purple as my dress.

He held out his hands as if to offer them to me, but then

I saw that they were bound by rope and one long, fast-growing tendril of Spanish moss. Both his palms cupped a fistful of pills.

"Unbind me," he mouthed, his emerald-green eyes boring into me.

"NO!" I screamed.

Principal Glass chuckled into the microphone. "Now, Natalie, don't be modest. I've had the honor to preview your documentary tonight, and I can safely say that we are all in for a very special treat."

"He's here. He's watching us," I wailed. Why wasn't anyone doing anything about J.B.? "He's going to—"

Mike stood up and put his arm around me. "She means Justin," he explained calmly to the audience. "Of course, he's watching over us tonight, baby," he cooed loud enough for everyone to hear. "Nat's just exhausted. She's beside herself. We all are," Mike said, nodding.

I could hear the rest of the school whispering. My chest was sweating, and I could see red stars in front of my eyes. Before them, J.B. was hovering directly over our heads. He was reaching for Mike's crown.

"You can have it," I screamed, wrestling the crown from Mike's head. "Here, you can take mine, too!"

My crown had been fixed in my hair by an hour's careful placement of bobby pins and at least a can of hair spray. It was going to take all my strength and half of my hair follicles to yank it off my head.

But then, I'd be rid of it for good.

I threw both crowns like star-crossed Frisbees as far away as I could. In the breathless silence, they clattered on the stage in front of us.

"I can't breathe," I said, clutching my throat. "I took off the crown, and I still can't breathe. What else do you want from me?"

Then Mike hoisted me up in his arms and started carrying me offstage.

"Enjoy the film," he called over his shoulder to the audience.

"What's happening to you?" he whispered when we were alone behind the curtain.

I looked back toward the stage and could hear Principal Glass nervously stammer, "Everyone please remain calm," just as my crown came to a rolling stop in the middle of the stage.

CHAPTER *Eighteen*

THAT WHICH WE DESTROY

"Is my crown in there?" I asked the nice lady hunched over the trashcan behind school on Monday morning. I'd never seen anyone other than students out here before, but it was nice to have a companion.

"Find your own treasure chest, Princess," she snarled at me. "This is my turf."

When she stuffed her head back inside the bin, I noticed she was wearing an oversize nylon tracksuit and the kind of flip-flops they give you after you get a pedicure. But I still envied the determination in her voice. She knew what she wanted. She knew what was rightfully hers. It reminded me of someone I used to know. . . .

"Hey." She popped back up again, holding the dirty carcass of a fish, wagging it like a finger in my face. "Aren't you the kiddo who won that little contest, Queen or something? Shouldn't you be inside, in class?"

I sniffed, inhaling the all too familiar fishy odor. "I was just looking for my crown," I said. "I lost it."

"Here." She cackled, digging through the bin. "Wear this."

She pulled out a jester hat, trashed after someone's Mardi Gras party, and tossed it at me. It was coated in something green and sour-smelling and it landed on my chest with a moist thump. I peeled the hat off my old Palmetto sweatshirt and held it out in front of me.

"Suits you," she burped, before digging into a bucket of chicken tossed into the trashcan. "If you'll excuse me, it's breakfast time."

"Sure," I nodded, dropping the hat. I heard a bell ringing in the distance—then remembered: I still had to go to school.

I was Natalie Hargrove, and I was kicking off my first week as fallen Palmetto Princess by taking fashion cues from the dispossessed.

"Ugh," I said, dropping the hat and racing inside to wash my hands.

"God, what is that smell?" Kate Richards said, holding her nose when I barged into the closest bathroom.

"Shut up, Bambies," I said, lumping Kate right in with the rest of them. I turned on the hot water. "Just move."

"Sick. Gladly," Steph Merritt said, backing away. "Do you want to borrow a brush or something?" she asked.

I looked at myself in the mirror. Maybe it had been a few days since my last shower. I guess my roots did look like you could toss a salad in them. And this sweatshirt, even with the green-jester-hat stain, still didn't really match my dark green jeans. And I knew if my mom could see my splotchy foundation right now, I would probably be grounded.

But I wasn't taking charity from anyone—not the bums outside, not the Bambies with their brushes.

"I'm fine," I lied, for about the hundredth time since my breakdown at the Ball on Friday.

It had been a long weekend. Mike came by, but I wouldn't see him. The phone rang and I turned it off. My mom knocked and I locked the door. All I could do was watch our original "Path to Palmetto" DVD on loop and obsess over what might have gone down at the Ball after I'd left.

Also: I wasn't sure how to erase the fact that I had seen a ghost. It seemed like only a matter of time before J.B. returned to haunt me again—forever.

This morning came too quickly, and now it was starting to dawn on me that I had two identities: There was the Natalie these Bambies saw before them—ragged, strung out, and unbathed. The fallen. And then there was the real me—the one consumed by nothing other than waiting for J.B. to come back.

I left the bathroom and walked numbly down the hall. Was I really going to go to my first class, sit down, and open my embossed Palmetto binder to take notes? Was I really going to sit thought another week's rumor mill?

"Nat." I felt a hand tap the back of my shoulder. It was Amy Jane, looking worried. "I've been calling you all weekend."

I nodded, holding my tongue.

"I'm trying to organize a viewing party for your 'Path to Palmetto' film, and I need to get your availability."

"That won't be necessary," I murmured.

"Of course, it is. You and Mike worked so hard on P2P. To have your big moment cut short just because you had a badly timed drop in blood sugar . . . um, is that split pea soup on your sweatshirt?"

"Wait." My head shot up. "What did you say? They didn't air the movie Friday night?"

"'Course not." Amy shrugged. "It didn't seem right without the royal couple. After you fainted, the rest of us just kind of tapered out." She leaned in. "Are you okay? Your pupils look a little dilated."

"You're telling me Ari didn't play it?" I gripped the straps of my backpack for support.

Amy Jane nodded, concertedly biting her lip.

So all the old enemies still stood. Nothing had been accomplished Friday night. And now, it was only a matter of time before Baxter reared his doped-up head again. With Kate Richards's fickle track record, he could easily lure her in again. Worse, I had no collateral to coerce Officer Parker to nab Baxter instead of me. There had been one shining moment Friday night when all the stars seemed aligned to keep Mike and me afloat. Because of J.B.'s ghost, everything we had going for us had slipped right through our fingers. We'd have to start all over. At this point, I knew we didn't have a chance.

"So I can pencil you in for Wednesday at four, Thursday at six, or Friday at—Nat?" Amy Jane called after me. "Where are you going?"

I turned the corner to the hallway where Mike and all the other football players had their lockers. His was empty.

"Where's Mike?" I said to the next group of students I passed. I didn't know any of their names, but they would know me and they would know who my boyfriend was. But instead of giving me any kind of helpful answer, the whole crowd of them scooted nervously away from me, backing up against the lockers.

"We don't know," one of them cried. "Don't hurt us."

"Didn't anyone ever tell you that what you don't know *can* hurt you," I spit and kept walking.

"Ms. Hargrove, a word?" It was the secretary, Mrs. Runner, sticking her head around a corner out of nowhere. I jumped like I'd seen a ghost all over again.

"A word?" I repeated. "*Deposed.*"

"Excuse me?"

"Is there any other word?"

She scratched her chin. "I really couldn't say. But Principal Glass would like to see you in his office," she said. "Now."

"I—" I looked over her shoulder through the fishbowl glass dividers and saw Officer Parker in a huddle with the principal. Another policeman was there as well.

My heart started hammering so hard I could barely think. Was it over? Did they know?

"I can't," I finally said, taking a step backward, and then another. "I have . . . another meeting."

"Excuse me?" Mrs. Runner said. As thankless as her job was, I guess she wasn't used to being told no by a student.

"Tell Glass I'll have to take a rain check," I said, quickly walking past her. "Sorry."

Actually, I did have another meeting. There was only one person I could think of who might be able to help shake me out of this haunted cloud. I headed upstairs to the junior bathroom, taking the stairs two at a time.

"Tracy," I said, barging in the door. A cluster of whispering juniors broke up and looked at me. "I need to see you."

Suddenly, there were a whole lot of pierced raised eyebrows in the room.

Tracy was sitting cross-legged on the floor. She'd released her long black hair from its braids, and now it grazed the ground. Her sapphire sunglasses seemed to place a barrier between us that was icier than normal. She looked at her watch. "Sorry, the bell's about to ring."

"Skip class," I said flatly.

"I'm reading cards for someone else right now," she said coolly. "Why don't you come back during lunch?"

"I don't think so; I'm here now." I dared not glance in the mirror again, but I suddenly wondered if holding my ground and pulling my senior privilege was less effective when I looked the way I did.

We faced off for a good thirty seconds, until the other juniors started to get uncomfortable, packing up their hemp bags and pulling on their dreads.

"You know what, Tracy?" Portia Stead said, shrugging her bare brown shoulders. "We can just come back next break."

"No," Tracy said, sounding nervous. "Why don't you all stay—"

But the girls quickly filed out of the bathroom and soon, Tracy and I were alone. She shook her head at me.

"What happened to you?" she asked. She said it not with disgust the way the Bambies had this morning, or even the way Mike had on Friday night. Tracy asked with genuine wonder.

"I don't know," I admitted, lowering myself into one of the beanbag on the floor. It felt so good to relax, to sink back and close my eyes.

"Cut the cards," she said.

When I opened my eyes, she was holding out a tarot deck. I'd seen her do readings for other girls, lots of times, but I'd never really bought into it. Her prophecies to me always came via word of mouth, Tracy just seemed to know how to get the gossip first and vet it for lies better than anyone else at Palmetto. But if she wanted to get into the heavier stuff today, I wasn't going to argue.

I reached forward and cut the deck in half, leaving it for her to deal. I almost expected to feel some sort of magic tingle when I touched them, but it was just like we were playing old maid or go fish.

Tracy lined up six cards in two rows of three. She stared at them for a few minutes, running her fingers along the edges. Her lips were moving, but no sound came out. The bell rang and neither of us moved.

"I don't know what you did," she said finally. "But you have a very guilty conscience." She squinted and rubbed her forehead. "Things were going well for you, but you took advantage of someone, someone vulnerable."

My throat felt parched. I couldn't swallow. She looked up at me. "This isn't me talking here, Nat, okay?"

She cleared her throat. "You're, uh . . . you're running out of people you can trust."

"Well, tell me what to do," I said. "Just look at the cards and tell me how I can fix things. I can still get them back."

Tracy bit her lip. "Some of them are already gone," she said slowly.

"You have to help me, Tracy. I trust you."

She shrugged and shook her head. "I can't tell you anything else, Nat. I only see what's in the cards."

"Read them again," I offered. "Here, I'll cut."

"You know it doesn't work that way."

"I don't," I insisted. "I don't know anything anymore."

"You know how to take drastic measures," she said. "Clearly. You'll figure out what you have to do to get out of this." She cocked her head. "Or else you won't. But I think, this time, you really are on your own."

A car horn beeped outside, and Tracy looked at her watch again.

"Now, I really have to go," she said, standing up. "You of all people know how a man hates to be kept waiting."

I thought about Mike, whom I'd more or less kept waiting all weekend. And now that I was finally ready to turn to him, he was nowhere to be found. I needed to know if I'd really blown it with him after Friday night, but by the time the question formed in my mind, Tracy had already slid open the window and was starting to shimmy out.

"Wait—" I called.

She shimmied step by step down a couple of bricks, lowered her feet, and leaped to the ground one story below, and as she did, her sunglasses slipped down to the tip of her nose. When she glanced up at me, I realized, I had never seen her eyes before. Her irises were a wild smoky purple color, and there was something about them that was almost . . . hazy, like clouds passing over the bay after a storm.

She offered me one final long and exaggerated wink, then snapped the glasses back up over her luminous eyes. A second later, she was slinking through the Cyprus trees toward the street.

A white camper was stalled in the driveway, and she pulled open the door and climbed in. I was fifty feet away and looking through a window that might not have been cleaned in the history of our school, but it was still clear that the camper Tracy climbed into now was the very same camper Slutsky had climbed into at the bar the other night. The trading post for drugs sure got around. My heart plummeted even further at the thought of the rumor mill catching whiff of the fact that I'd had J.B.'s antiseizure pills. I was running out of notches on the paranoia belt, and what was worse, I had finally run out of people to turn to.

There wasn't anyone left to trust, except myself.

CHAPTER *Nineteen*

SLEEP NO MORE

No trail of bread crumbs or boxers this time, I went to the waterfall alone. The encounter with Tracy in the bathroom this morning had left me paralyzed. Her stormy eyes were haunting me, and my mind couldn't stop running over all the prophecies she'd given. She'd been right about Mike winning Palmetto Prince. She'd been right about revenge being close (though as it turned out, it was J.B. who got revenge and not me). She'd even been right today, that I was absolutely out of options and utterly on my own. The only prediction that hadn't yet come to pass was the mention of "the fall" following the revenge. I still couldn't figure out exactly what that one meant—which was what had led me here tonight.

It was raining again, and the path uphill was muddy and steep. I grabbed at Cyprus branches for support as I climbed and stepped over the Venus flytraps coating the way. I had never been scared to hike alone at night, but I was trembling now.

Maybe it would help to remember that I had nothing left to lose.

At the top of the path, a hoot owl greeted me, looking like a fat black cat in the spruce tree. I ducked under the low hanging branch and stepped inside the water-carved stone cave. It was the first time I'd ever been to the waterfall without Mike—and the first time I think I ever really saw what it looked like. Every other time we'd come, the destination was just a backdrop for us. Tonight, the alcove felt cramped and dangerous, everything slippery, wet, and cold.

I stood at the ledge, where I used to love to tower over Mike, making him nervous if I got close enough to the edge so that the water ran down my hair. Now when I looked out over the edge, I was overcome by vertigo. I sat back down in the nook to breathe.

I was safe here. I was finally safe and alone. It was a feeling that I planned on getting used to.

I had a plan. I knew what I had to do.

It wouldn't be right to not say good-bye to Mike, though. My heart clenched just thinking about it. How could I face him? And yet, how to express all that we'd done wrong? How to account for where I ended up after tonight? How to caution him on where he should go from here?

As much as you can understand, you will.
—Always, Natalie

No apologies, which were more often unwanted than too little or too late. He would get it from the note I'd left in his locker. If he didn't—

There was his face. He was all over the scrapbook I'd brought with me in my backpack.

I hadn't meant to crack it open here; it was just one of those things I couldn't leave behind. Suddenly, I was poring over our lives together, tearing through the delicate pages, looking for some kind of answer.

We'd grown up in a three-year long embrace, and as careful as I'd been about documenting it, I guess I'd never really taken the time to look through the album after I had put it together. It was funny; most of the pictures had been taken from the same angle, with the camera only ever as far away as one of our arms could reach. It was like we'd been too consumed by each other to let go long enough to ask someone else to take the picture.

I didn't know which one of us had let go first these past weeks. All I knew now was that it was cold here with the steady mist of water fogging up the plastic cover on the album's pages. My fingers trembled, turning blue as I flipped through them. At the back of the book, ten blank pages—bookmarked and reserved for pictures I'd meant to take of us at Palmetto Court on Friday night.

Let them stay blank. At least they'd be purer that way. At least they'd just be little white lies.

Once, in freshman composition class, we did a writing exercise: Pretend your house is burning, and you only have minutes to escape. What five things would you grab on your way out the door?

It's supposed to teach you what you value, what cannot be replaced. It's supposed to suggest that you'd know what mattered to you instantly, in the heat of the moment. I used to wonder what it was about. Why did it take your whole world going up in flames before you got that kind of clarity?

Once, I would have brought my Jessamine, stuffed and wrinkled in the backpack, but things had turned out differently than I expected them to. Where I was going now, there'd be no use for a giant silk flower, dangling ribbons, the rare crown charm.

My hands were shaking. I closed the scrapbook and reached into my bag for the one thing I knew would calm me down.

"Nat, what are you doing?"

It was Mike. He ducked under the tree branch to join me.

"What are *you* doing?" I said, dropping the backpack.

"You weren't at school; you weren't at home. I started to get a bad feeling,"

Mike's black raincoat was dripping when he took it off and tossed it on the ground. Outside, the hoot owl flew the coop.

"You shouldn't have come here," I said.

Mike sighed and crossed his arms. He was leaning against the stone slab on the other side of the alcove. He felt too close to me, too stifling, and at the same time, too far away.

"Nat, I got a call today," he said, looking everywhere but at me. "It was from your dad."

"That's impossible," I said, and even then my mind began to race to come up with a quick explanation, a way out. But I was so tired. It was over.

"I'm not mad," Mike said. He sat down next to me and reached for my hand. "It sounds crazy, but a lot of things finally make sense. I even understand why you lied."

I shook my hand away. "You don't know anything about why I did what I did. You don't know anything about me."

"Your dad told me a lot more than you ever would have," he said. "He said he's been trying to reconnect with you."

For a second, I wondered how exactly my dad would have summed up our sordid past. Would he have told Mike about the two years he pretended to go to work every day at the wharf and ended up slumped over at the bar? Or how far he'd come since the day his buddies at the station slapped a pair of handcuffs on his wrists? Mike might be a novice when it came to being conned by my father, but I'd believed his apologies and vows to change too many times to walk into one more letdown.

"You don't know my father," I said resolutely. "He's a con artist, Mike."

"He's worried about you," he said. "I guess we have that in common."

I stood up, pacing the small stone ledge. I couldn't believe we were even having this conversation. It was almost a shame that I was never going to see my dad again, that I was never going to have the chance to chew him out for this.

"Mike, you can't just believe everything everyone tells you. He didn't call you because he was worried about me," I said. "My guess is he called when he caught wind of your trust fund."

Mike shook his head. "You're upset," he said. He tried to put his arms around me. "You're just tired and upset."

I pushed him off. "You're *unconscious.*"

Now Mike's face flushed, and he stepped forward, towering over me.

"I'm 'unconscious?'" he asked. "I was the one who wanted to own up to what happened from the beginning. I'm not the one who spent my whole life running away from my past."

"Why should you?" I spit. "You're Mike King. You have no

idea what it's like to need to run away."

Speaking of which—

It was time to go. I had wanted to leave Charleston on some sort of a high note. I'd wanted one peaceful parting gesture at the waterfall, but now that Mike had shown up and made that an impossibility, I just wanted to get out as soon as possible. I reached down and picked up my backpack, stuffing the scrapbook inside.

"What's this?" Mike asked, pulling it out of my hands. The album fell open to a picture of the two of us in this very spot at a much more innocent time in our relationship. He looked up me. His eyes started to water. "Why did you bring this here?" he asked. "What else do you have in that bag?"

"Nothing," I muttered. "Just leave me alone."

"Natalie, what's going on?" He grabbed for the backpack at my shoulder, but I kept a firm grip on the straps. After a split second of tug-of-war, I felt the zipper give way. It split down the middle, exposing the gaping insides of the bag like a purple Venus flytrap. About twenty packs of Juicy Fruit ricocheted in all directions, and I gasped as the one thing I really hadn't wanted Mike to see floated through the air and landed at his feet.

He reached down to pick it up. I held my breath. He swallowed hard as his eyes ran over my one-way bus ticket to New York.

His brow furrowed. He looked at his watch and said,

"Cutting it a little close to departure time, don't you think?"

"Mike."

I stepped toward him, but he pushed me away. I stumbled backward, up against the wall. His hands felt so rough on my chest.

"Let me guess," he said, with a venom in his voice I'd never heard before. "I don't get it, right? Tortured, complicated Nat and her gullible trust-fund boyfriend. Is that what you think?"

Once, I would have fallen on him and begged for his mouth on mine so we'd stop saying things we didn't mean. The awful thing was, by now, we meant everything we were saying.

"Leave me alone," I said. "Just put my things down and leave me alone."

"No," he folded up the ticket and stuffed it in his pocket. "You think you can just disappear and what we did will disappear, too? I won't let you leave me, Nat. Not with all of this."

"You'll be better off without me," I said, knowing that what I meant was that we'd both be better off. No one would pin this all on Mike alone, and maybe somewhere, far away, there could be a fresh start for me, too. "Give me my ticket," I said, holding out my hand.

"No."

Mike crossed his arms over his chest. I had no other

choice. I came at him one last time. And one last time, he shoved me back.

Only this time, he was just forceful enough to make a difference. This time, I didn't stop stumbling backward until there wasn't any more ground to stumble on. My foot clipped over the edge of the waterfall, and Mike and I locked eyes.

We knew. Right then, both of us knew exactly what was going to happen.

His hand reached out for mine. It was too late.

In a way, hadn't it always been too late for Mike and me? Sure, I had tried to make a fresh start when I crossed over to Palmetto, but I guess some pasts are just too powerful. Mine had a way of creeping up on me. I could only fight it for so long before I fell.

When it came, I let it happen. You could say I even welcomed it, falling backward with as much grace as I could muster, through the sheet of ice-cold water, then down with it. Down into the still, black pool below.

CHAPTER *Twenty*

YOUNG IN DEED

Some say your life flashes before your eyes just before you die. For me, it was just one moment. Same water, different fall.

I was thirteen years old and about to go skinny-dipping for the very first time.

"Hurry up," Sarah called from the other side of the hemlock patch. "It'll be warmer once we get in the water."

She'd already left her clothes in a heap next to me. I looked down at her flimsy pink bra, her cut-off shorts, the white wifebeater tank top she'd bought in a three pack at the drugstore. I pictured what she must look like on the other side of the bush, naked except for her flip-flops and the shark-tooth necklace she always wore. The tattoo on the small of her back would look bright against her pale skin in the moonlight. She'd be shivering and hugging her arms around her chest. You could hear it in her voice: She couldn't wait to get in the water with the boys.

I was nervous. I didn't know these guys whom she'd met in the movie theater parking lot on the other side of town when she'd been on a date with someone else. The way she told the story, one of them rolled down the window of his red Camero, and she was sliding through it before he even finished suggesting that she ditch her date for someone with a faster ride.

"We're talking about guys from Palmetto," she'd told me later that night on the phone. "They drive fast, they talk fast, and they move fast. They're not like anyone we know."

It wasn't long before she convinced me to go with her to meet them behind one of their houses on the Cove. Whoever it was, it wasn't even his main house, Sarah raved to me; it was an extra weekend house, like something only movie stars had.

We had to hitchhike to get there, our bathing suits and our cuter clothes tucked in a beach bag so no one from our neighborhood would think anything of it if they saw us on the street. It was one thing to sneak out and stay in Cawdor; it was another thing to go over to Palmetto. People might start to imagine that you thought you were above where you came from.

The boys outnumbered us. They were bigger and older,

and their bathing suits probably cost twice as much as mine and Sarah's combined. I was embarrassed about my knock-off solid-color one-piece with the racer back that made me look even flatter than I was. Sarah saw it in my face.

"I have an idea," she sang.

Twenty minutes later, she was still waiting for me to build up the guts to take off my clothes and meet her on the dock. We were going to stand there for a minute in the moonlight, then dive in—just far enough from the guys that we'd be little more than silhouettes, just long enough that they'd get the gist.

Finally, she brushed back through the hemlock, took a hold of my shirt herself, and yanked it over my head.

"Hey," I teased. "I thought you were into guys."

We were both cracking up as she unzipped my jeans, and I kicked my legs free.

"About effing time," she grinned, sizing me up as I wrapped my arms around myself, shivering. "Hot. Okay, which one of the guys do you want? I'm starting with Tommy."

"Starting with?" I laughed.

"The night is young, honey," she shrugged dramatically. I was starting to understand why my mom and her friends called Sarah's mom a whore, a label that took a lot to earn, especially in the type of trailer park circles Mom ran in. But to me, Sarah's eagerness was a rush. She was the first girl I'd ever seen who actually seemed in control of what she did with her body. If she wanted something, she got it. She was almost like a guy.

I realized she was staring at me, waiting for me to call dibs on which one I wanted first.

"I don't really know any of these guys," I said. "How am I supposed to pick?"

"Good point," she agreed. "Get to know them in the water; it'll be sexier. Flash now, call dibs later, okay?"

I nodded, cracking a grin.

"Stick with me, Tal," she said, leading me outside. "I'll teach you everything you need to know."

I did, and she did. At least for a little while.

As soon as the first guy caught a glimpse of us naked on the dock getting ready to dive in, there was a flurry of splashing as the rest of them all swam out to meet us. Sarah and I held hands, raised them up over our heads, and dove into the water together.

When I came up for air, I was face to face with a blond-headed boy treading water. I hadn't seen him before in the crowd, but without a word, he treaded closer, brushed a hand against my face, and kissed me.

"I'm Justin," he said. "Call me J.B."

"Natalie," I gasped, trying to stay afloat. "Everyone calls me Tal."

"You've got a pretty face, Tal," he said. "And a pretty obscene body."

I had only been kissed twice before, never by someone whose name I didn't know, and I'd definitely never been spoken to like that. Now, there was this kid, who was younger than the rest of the guys by a few years—maybe my age—acting like he'd written all new rules.

"What do you say I show you my boat?" he asked. "I think you'll like it."

I glanced over at Sarah, who was splashing one of the guys playfully, her head thrown back in the air. She caught my eye and winked.

"Okay," I said to Justin.

He took my hand underwater, and we swam toward a marina where a row of shiny motorboats were docked. Justin pulled himself out of the water and onto the side of the boat. I couldn't help watching the way his body looked as he lifted up a seat compartment to grab a towel. He caught me staring, and when I dropped my head, he said, "It's okay. Get a good look. I plan to do the same when I help you up in a minute."

I was still blushing when he reached down and took both of my hands in his, pulling me up on the boat. I gasped from the feel of the cold air on my wet skin and from the realization that I was very naked and very alone with a stranger on the other side of town.

"Hmm, where is that extra towel?" he joked, scratching his chin.

"Oh my God," I said, covering myself with my hands, half terrified, half ecstatic. "You'd better give me your towel right now."

We wrestled for the one towel until I slipped, and Justin landed on top of me with a thud. He kissed me again, stroking my cheek with two fingers.

"So where do you go to school?" he said.

"You really want to talk about school?" I giggled. "Now?"

"I guess I want to get to know you. I dunno." Now he was the one who was blushing. Water churned under the boat, making me feel dizzy. But it was a good kind of dizzy.

"Christ," a voice muttered from behind us. "I guess we'd better warn lover boy over there."

I jerked away, pulling as much of the towel over me as I could. Two of the other guys were standing over us, both dripping wet, both with snide looks on their faces. Suddenly, it felt anything but okay to be naked on this boat.

"These girls aren't here to make conversation with, little bro," the tall one said. He looked like Justin but a few years older. He must be Tommy. "They are here to screw and then go home."

I gasped and all three of the guys turned to me.

"Aww," the other guy said. His dark wet hair hung down over his eyes. "Trailer trash is cute when she plays innocent."

Tommy nodded. "She might look better in the face, but she's no different from Slutsky over there."

I looked over to where I'd left Sarah. I could hear her having-the-time-of-my-life laugh ringing out across the water. And here was the guy we'd come all twenty miles to see, calling her Slutsky behind her back.

"Whatever," Justin said. "We're just hanging out, okay?"

"Turn around, trailer trash," Tommy told me.

"Her name's Tal," Justin said.

"I said turn around, trailer trash," Tommy said louder. "I want to see your tramp stamp."

"What?" I asked.

"Every bitch from Cawdor gets the same slut tattoo right above her ass. It's how guys like us know where to aim when we've got you—"

"Easy, Tommy," the other guy said.

"If he's going to hang with the big dogs, my little brother needs to understand a few things," Tommy insisted. "Let's see exhibit A."

"I don't have a tattoo," I said.

"No, shit?" Tommy asked, sizing me up. "Did Slutsky bring us a baby? How novel."

"Well, it's only a matter of time," the other guy sneered, fist-bumping Tommy.

He turned to Justin. "Just remember, these girls are good for three things." As he spoke, Tommy held up his fingers. "Taking it off, taking what you give them, then getting taken back across the bridge."

Justin looked at me then, and his eyes were different, like he blamed me for both of us being here, getting this lecture.

"Yeah," he said coldly. "I know."

"What?" I whispered.

"When you do get that old tramp stamp, let me know," Justin said, earning a cheer from the older guys.

I started toward him, without a plan, just knowing that everything Justin Balmer had said to lure me in had been a lie. But before I reached Justin, Tommy grabbed my wrists.

"Ohhh," he taunted. "Baby's getting feisty. Don't you worry, sweetheart," he cooed, his voice dripping condescension. Then he grabbed a fistful of towel at my waist and started pulling. "Here, let me show you how it's done."

In a panic, my eyes shot up at Justin. He looked away. Before Tommy could tug the last of my towel away, I channeled all the fear and humiliation in me and shoved it at him.

I didn't even stick around to watch him stumble back. I dove, naked, into the lake, letting the cold, black water flush away my tears. I forgot about Sarah; I forgot about my clothes. I just wanted to swim all the way back home.

By the time I started freshman year at Palmetto, I'd been through a whole lot worse than that frozen moment on the dock. I had longer hair, thicker skin, the right zip code and wardrobe, and a different nickname to prove that I had fully put that past behind me.

But the first time I saw J.B. in the halls of my new school, I was right back at that marina, totally exposed, totally worthless.

He passed me in the hall, then doubled back around. "You look familiar," he said, squinting. "Have we met?"

Epilogue

*O*nce, you used to envision your final exit from high
school, some fairy-tale ending to your story. You
were so easily won over by honest trifles. You succumbed so
quickly to the instruments of darkness, snapping your Juicy
Fruit, thinking you were on top of the world.

They spent nearly a week searching for Natalie Hargrove's
body, and Dotty Perch spent that long praying for her soul.
She went through box after box of tissues, flanked on either
side by Darla and the Dick on the couch at the hacienda by
the lake. The Dick combed through her hair with his fingers,
brewed her fourth pot of decaf hazelnut coffee. He could never
erase what had happened to Dotty's only daughter. The deed
was done. The battle was lost and won. But she had someone

to take care of her at last, and a house built from a lifetime of coveting. She would eventually find happiness. You would, too, if you were her.

The Double D was another story. She treated Natalie's old locker like her own personal wailing wall, her nubby fingers peeling at the poster taped across its red metal door.

The poster read: *Kate Richards, from Handmaiden to Princess. Discover Palmetto's brightest new star.*

As easily as Kate Richards filled the hole left by Natalie Hargrove, you might expect to find our bright new star on the arm of a certain reigning King. But no one at Palmetto had seen or heard from Mike since Natalie's tragic accident. Perhaps that one-way ticket out of town got put to use after all. . . .

Back at Palmetto, Officer Parker was making a personal discovery of his own. The cops had finally gotten around to cleaning out Justin Balmer's locker. Inside it, they'd found a football helmet, socks, jock straps. And a small zipper case.

Tucked into the case, were a handful of pictures.

Of Natalie Hargrove.

Natalie serving lemonade at the freshman fund-raiser.

Natalie by the flagpole tossing her head back to laugh, so that the sun sparkled in her long dark hair.

Natalie's jeweled lilac dress glinting in the light from the snow globe at last year's winter formal.

And more. Photos of Nat across all four years they'd spent at Palmetto.

Proof that there was more to J.B. than anyone knew, buried truths behind his emerald-green eyes. Proof that things aren't always what you think they are.

Once, you imagined you could be anyone you wanted to be. That you could make the right guy love you and rescue you from your fate. That you could outsmart everyone and leave your past behind for good.

How hard you worked for what you wanted.

How cruelly fate betrayed you in the end.

Turn the page for a chapter from the new Razorbill series by NANCY HOLDER:

POSSESSIONS

one

October 28

possessions: me

- Tibetan prayer beads
- Mem's UCSD sweatshirt
- used black leather boho bag (thrift shop in Poway)
- Converse high-tops (from Target)
- Dad's socks (too big, but they're his)
- tattered jeans (origin forgotten)
- tortoiseshell headband (plastic)
- NO makeup
- five single-subject notebooks
- regulation Marlwood Academy planner
- ditto binder
- six #2 pencils, one missing eraser (panic attack)
- pens (unlimited)
- cell phone (no bars, no reception here AT ALL)
- Jason's St. Christopher medal (thanks, Cuz!)
- me, Lindsay 2.0 (or so I hope)

haunted by: my past

listening to: my heartbeat—too fast again! *don't forget to breathe.*

mood: frozen to death (not a mood?!)

possessions: them

oh.

my.

God.

is there anything they DON'T have???

haunted by: not seeing any haunting

listening to: each other

mood: excited? they can pay for any mood they want.

———

Fog had crawled up the mountain, like a wounded animal on pine-tree claws, and bled all over the campus. I stopped and squinted at my map with its handy printed stats—a hundred developed acres that included hiking paths and bike trails; thirty buildings, including a brick gym with a plaster frieze, which really needed updating, of ancient Greek athletes (male)—who could also have used some underwear, if I remembered the picture correctly.

The campus was rolling in white mist, and I wasn't sure of the way to the classrooms, which were clustered on the north side of the campus. I had thought there was a shortcut through

Academy Quad, my quad, but it was hard to be sure when I couldn't see more than ten feet ahead of myself.

Then a stiff wind blew, thinning the fog. Sure enough, my building loomed on top of the small hill to my left. Grose was a creaky, scary-looking rectangle made out of brick, with a slate roof. Another dorm, Jessel, crouched at the bottom of the hill like it was waiting to pounce. It was three stories tall with a slight-L-shape, where a back porch jutted out like a hunchback.

Jessel was prettier than Grose. It had towering stone columns on either side of its brightly painted red front door, and four turret rooms, one on each corner, covered in slate shingles. The windows of the turrets were arched, completing the castle-tower effect.

Everyone else in both Grose and Jessel had already moved in, made friends, and started right on schedule—September 5th. I couldn't believe they'd let me start so late. Maybe nervous breakdowns came with benefits.

I was here to reinvent myself in a major way. No one here *knew* I had gone bonkers. No one here knew me at all. I could be anyone—Lindsay Anne Cavanaugh 2.0. I really hoped I would like the remix better. I was optimistic; I had started out well as a person—had normal friends, liked animals, did pretty well in school. I used to kick butt on the cello. Okay, my mom died. And Jane Taylor seduced my boyfriend. In our house. On the throw I knitted for my mom in the hospital.

And yeah, I'd pretended I didn't care. I'd acted like it was no big deal. Because I wanted to be one of Jane's cool chicks.

That was called cognitive dissonance, when you wanted two

opposing things—such as self-respect and popularity. A broken heart and a shot at riding in Jane's limo to Homecoming.

A second chance and all my insecurities begging me to get the heck out of here. . . .

Sometimes, wanting those two opposing things made you fracture, like two tectonic plates crashing together beneath the surface of the ocean.

"So what do you think, Botox? Or a deal with the Devil? I heard Ehrlenbach's sixty-eight." A girl's voice wafted out of the billows of horror-movie white. I placed her at maybe twenty yards to my right—my Jessel side, where a private hedge hid their front yard from view. Dr. Ehrlenbach was our headmistress, and I had yet to meet her.

"Did you spend your summer in rehab? No one does Botox anymore," someone else shot back. "But if she's really that old, my money's on the Devil. My dad would do her in a heartbeat. I've heard him say so. All right, blindfold her."

I blinked. Slowed. Waited to hear more.

"That's too tight. Ow," a third voice protested.

"You know, Keeks, you don't have to do this," the second voice said, but there was a silent *but you'd better* tacked on the end, sharpened with the familiar edge of an accomplished bitch. I knew then and there that I was eavesdropping not only on a mean girl, but a leader of same—a queen bee. I was an expert on queen bees. Unfortunately.

Nothing to see here, Lindsay, I told myself, as my face prickled from memories and apprehension. *Move it along. Even better, run.*

They could have their fun. I was not there to have fun of any kind, especially that kind.

"I'm not so sure about this." That was Keeks again.

"Tie her hands." Her Majesty.

Yow.

"Maybe we'd better wait." The first girl I'd heard. Not in charge.

"Just do it, Lara. Oh, forget it. Give me the rope and—"

"God, Mandy, chill. I'm on it."

Mandy. How typical. I wondered if Mandy was half as mean as Jane; and if she was, I pitied Lara just for being there almost as much as I pitied Keeks, whoever she was, for agreeing to be blindfolded and tied up in the middle of a fog bank when they should be in class. Obviously, Keeks had to prove herself to get into their exclusive little club. So not worth it.

By then I was at the hedge. *Just a peek*, I told myself, *just to make sure she's okay.*

The privet leaves were wet and small, covering branches that grew together as dense as an actual fence. I smelled wet earth and my own sugar-free cinnamon gum. Wind toyed with my crazed ringlets as I raised myself up on my tiptoes in an attempt to peer out of a thinned-out space above my head. I'm only five-foot-two, and it was out of my reach. I crept to my left, still unable to see anything.

"Let's get started. Breathe in, breathe out, center. We gather to welcome you. Kiyoko, let go, let go of yourself, and become one of us." Nervous laughter drifted from a thinned section in the hedge, a circle of broken branch endings that looked as if someone had clipped them, like wire cutters on a chain-link fence. The opening emitted fog—as if *it* were breathing—and it creeped me out. I hugged my UCSD sweatshirt around myself as I moved in quietly and peered through. My high-tops sank into mud.

"Come to me, come to me," Mandy urged.

The fog rolled and churned; then I saw them. Two girls flanked a third, who was blindfolded. The tallest wore her light, nearly white-blonde hair in a messy bun. She had to be Mandy. Her full lips were curved in a smile I knew well—calculating, cruel, enjoying the distress of her victim.

Maybe-Mandy's neck was fashion-model long, and she was wearing glittering diamond earrings as big as pencil erasers. I assumed they were real. Her clothes were so fine—a long black coat hung open, revealing a knee-length black cashmere sweater-dress over black pencil-leg woolen trousers above high-heeled boots—and I saw a thick gold bangle around her wrist as she smoothed a wisp of hair away from her cheek. Everything looked designer and real.

"Become one of us," Mandy said again, her voice papery, and she exhaled, sending condensed breath all over the blindfolded girl's face.

"Become one of us," the other girl—Lara—chanted. She was grinning like a coyote that had stumbled on a nest of baby rabbits. Her emerald eyes (definitely contacts) gleamed as Kiyoko stood statue still. Lara was a classic redhead with ivory skin and a few cute freckles, her hair short and her clothes tasteful but boho—a man's plaid suit jacket in olive green and chocolate-brown, an extra-long white shirt, and the skinniest of skinny dark jeans.

Standing blindfolded in the center, Kiyoko's hands were tied behind her back, which was the part that made me extra-uneasy for her. It was going a little too far.

Kiyoko was rail-thin, the kind of thin that was too thin even for a model, and black silky hair cascaded over her shoulders. A gorgeous silvery sweater grazed the thighs of her gray jeans, but it hung too loose on her. Her legs were like sticks. She was chewing her lower lip; her golden-hued features displayed her concentration and eagerness.

"Become one of us," Mandy and Lara whispered together, their breaths spiraling up toward the sky.

Fog rushed all around me, wrapping me up in cold sheets of blank whiteness, and I couldn't see a thing. The chill seeped through my clothes straight through to my bones, and I shivered, hard. It felt as if the cold were creeping under my hair, straight into my *brain*.

I shuddered, and for a few seconds, I couldn't even think. For a quick moment, I thought I smelled . . . smoke? Then the sensation passed. Another strong wind whipped through the fog and thinned it out again—just as Mandy and Lara both stiffened and quickly inhaled. Their faces went slack, with their eyes still open.

I wondered if they were having some kind of infectious seizure. I waited for them to exhale, but it wasn't happening. Then I realized *I* was holding my breath, too, and forced myself to let it out. I felt shaky and weird.

I almost called out to see if they needed help. Before I went nuts, I had done some lifeguarding, and I was still certified in CPR.

Slowly, Mandy turned her head in my direction, as if she knew I was there. Probably not a good thing, spying. Before I realized what I was doing, I stepped to the right, where the branches grew closer together, blocking her view, although I could still see her sick little game.

Mandy's forehead creased in apparent frustration. I squinted as more fog rolled between us; when it wafted out of the way, her eyes looked completely black. No pupils. No white. No color. Just black.

Whoa, how high was she?

"Number Three," she intoned, and her voice sounded different. "Come to me." Higher, shriller, with a little Southern accent. Her laugh was high-pitched, and a tad OOC . . .

"Number three, come to me," Lara added, and her voice didn't sound the same either. Maybe a little lower . . . meaner . . .

"I'm here," Kiyoko murmured. She sounded unsure, more like she wanted to please them than anything else.

A deep chill ran through me, the fog moist and cold on my face. What exactly was I witnessing?

Then someone tapped me on the back, and I gasped and whirled around.